The Book of Endless Stories

Diversity, Equality, and Inclusion

Maya Roberts

Published by Whimsy Tales Press, 2024.

This is a work of fiction. Similarities to real people, places, or events are entirely coincidental.

THE BOOK OF ENDLESS STORIES

First edition. November 20, 2024.

Copyright © 2024 Maya Roberts.

ISBN: 979-8230721260

Written by Maya Roberts.

Table of Contents

Preface 1
Chapter 1: The Gateway of Stories 2
Chapter 2: The River of Kindness 6
Chapter 3: The Tree of Many Colors 9
Chapter 4: The Whispering Forest 13
Chapter 5: The Sky of Dreams 16
Chapter 6: The Garden of Forgotten Voices 20
Chapter 7: The Bridge of Understanding 24
Chapter 8: The Mountain of Courage 27
Chapter 9: The Circle of Trust 31
Chapter 10: The Dance of Respect 34
Chapter 11: The Valley of Forgiveness 38
Chapter 12: The Song of Belonging 41
Chapter 13: The Hidden Garden of Wonder 45
Chapter 14: The Workshop of Dreams 50
Chapter 15: The Lake of Reflection 53
Chapter 16: The Market of Generosity 57
Chapter 17: The Forest of Resilience 61
Chapter 18: The Tower of Understanding 65
Chapter 19: The Fountain of Kindness 69
Chapter 20: The Harbor of Peace 72
Chapter 21: The Garden of Curiosity 75
Chapter 22: The Cave of Dreams 79
Chapter 23: The River of Change 83
Chapter 24: The Path of Compassion 87
Chapter 25: The Horizon of Unity 91

Preface

As we journey through life, we encounter countless stories that shape who we are. *The Book of Endless Stories* was born from the belief that every culture, every person, and every experience contributes a unique piece to the grand mosaic of humanity. In this book, children will accompany Maya, a young explorer, as she journeys into diverse worlds, each teaching her valuable lessons about empathy, courage, unity, and respect. Through gentle and captivating adventures, young readers will learn that kindness is a universal language, that diversity is our strength, and that compassion is a bridge that brings us together. Each chapter encourages children to view the world with open hearts and inquisitive minds, understanding that the bonds we share are what make life's journey so beautiful. This book is a gentle invitation to explore, learn, and cherish the stories that connect us all.

Chapter 1: The Gateway of Stories

Maya was spending the weekend with her grandparents, a cozy escape she looked forward to every month. Their house was a treasure chest of stories. Every corner had a piece of history, from her grandmother's meticulously arranged trinkets to her grandfather's endless collection of old books. Their home was a place where time seemed to slow down, and all that mattered was the warmth of family and the thrill of discovery. One rainy afternoon, as Maya wandered into her grandfather's library, she stumbled upon a book she had never seen before.

The book had an unusual, thick leather cover and a title etched in fading golden letters: *The Book of Endless Stories*. It looked ancient, and there was something mesmerizing about it. Maya's fingers traced the letters as she whispered the title out loud. It seemed to hum with an energy all its own. She hesitated, a spark of curiosity dancing within her, and finally opened the cover, flipping to the first page. To her surprise, instead of words, she saw what looked like an endless forest of trees reaching up into a purple-hued sky. In a blink, the room disappeared around her, and she found herself standing at the edge of that very forest.

Confused but captivated, Maya stepped forward, her feet sinking into soft, moss-covered ground. The forest around her was alive, not just with the typical rustling of leaves but with a low hum, almost like a distant song, filling the air. It felt welcoming, like the forest itself was calling to her. In the midst of her awe, a gentle voice broke the silence.

"Hello, young one," it said.

Maya turned to see an old owl perched on a low branch. Its feathers were an array of soft browns and whites, and its eyes gleamed like polished amber. Maya had never seen such an owl, wise and ancient as if it had been watching over the forest for centuries.

"Hello," Maya replied, still astonished by her surroundings.

"I am Ori, the Keeper of Stories," the owl introduced itself with a slight bow. "And you, Maya, have opened the gateway."

Maya's eyes widened. How did this owl know her name? She hadn't spoken it aloud, had she?

"This forest," Ori continued, "is the beginning of many stories, stories that have been collected from places far and near, times long ago, and even from places that have yet to be. Each story holds a lesson, a truth, or a piece of wisdom."

Maya felt a thrill run through her. She loved stories, especially those with magic and mystery. But this was different; she felt as though she was actually part of the story.

"Will you come with me?" Ori asked, extending a wing toward a path that wound deeper into the forest.

Maya nodded eagerly. She followed Ori through the trees, each one towering above her with twisted branches stretching out like welcoming arms. The leaves shimmered in hues she couldn't describe, shades that didn't exist back in her world. As they walked, she noticed smaller creatures—a fox with silver fur, a deer with antlers that sparkled like frost—watching them from a distance, as though they, too, were aware of her presence.

Finally, they reached a small clearing where an ancient tree stood, its trunk as wide as three people standing arm in arm. At its base was an opening, dark but inviting, and Ori led her inside. As she entered, the space began to glow softly. Shelves carved into the walls were filled with scrolls, books, and artifacts, each one radiating a quiet magic. Ori gestured to a small, carved wooden bench.

"Sit, Maya," he said. "Let me tell you the first story."

She sat down, excitement bubbling up inside her, and Ori began to tell a tale that seemed to paint itself in the air. Colors swirled around them, forming images of a young child with an adventurous spirit not unlike her own. This child lived in a village nestled at the foot of a mountain, surrounded by rivers and forests. But in this village, there was a peculiar custom: each person wore a single color that represented them and their gifts to the community. Red for the brave, blue for the wise, green for the compassionate, yellow for the joyful, and purple for the dreamers.

One day, a young boy in the village decided he wanted to wear all the colors. He admired bravery, wisdom, compassion, joy, and dreams equally, feeling that each quality was essential. But the village elders shook their heads, insisting that he must choose just one. Torn and unsure, the boy wandered into the forest, hoping to find an answer. As he walked, he met a butterfly whose wings bore every color of the rainbow. The butterfly fluttered around him, shimmering with hues that captivated him.

"Why can you wear all the colors, but I cannot?" the boy asked the butterfly.

The butterfly laughed gently, saying, "I am a creature of many colors because I am free to be myself in all ways. I am both bold and gentle, joyful and thoughtful. My colors blend together, creating something new with each flap of my wings. Perhaps the village has forgotten that colors are meant to mix."

Inspired by the butterfly, the boy returned to the village and, despite the elders' words, crafted himself a garment with all the colors. At first, people were shocked, and some were angry. But soon, they began to see how he moved through the village, showing bravery, kindness, wisdom, joy, and dreams all at once. He reminded them that each color was a part of who they all were. Gradually, the villagers began to wear other colors too, realizing that they could embrace many qualities. And so, the boy's courage to be himself led the village into a new era, where everyone could celebrate their unique combinations of strengths.

Maya was entranced, feeling as though she, too, had met the colorful butterfly and watched the brave boy change his village. Ori's

THE BOOK OF ENDLESS STORIES

voice softened as the story came to an end, and the images faded back into the warm glow of the library.

Chapter 2: The River of Kindness

Maya couldn't shake the feeling of magic that lingered with her ever since she first opened *The Book of Endless Stories*. As she sat on her grandfather's porch the following day, the sky still heavy with rain clouds, she felt a familiar urge drawing her back to the old, leather-bound book. It sat innocently enough on her lap, yet she knew it held wonders beyond imagination. Taking a deep breath, she turned to the next page. Her fingers brushed over a delicate, water-colored illustration of a glistening river winding through hills, with small villages on either side. And just like that, with a soft whoosh and a sudden sensation of warmth, she found herself standing at the bank of that very river.

Maya looked around, taking in the stunning scene. The river stretched wide and calm, glistening under a gentle sun that peeked through wisps of mist. Its surface was smooth, almost mirror-like, reflecting the lush green hills and small cottages dotting the riverbanks. Villagers bustled about, tending to their homes, drawing water, and chatting in the gentle morning light. Though it felt like a place from another world, it also felt comfortingly familiar, as if she had been here before.

A soft hum reached her ears, almost like a melody carried on the breeze. Curious, she walked closer to the water's edge, where a group of children were gathering water in brightly painted pots. They chattered and laughed, greeting her warmly as if she was an old friend. Maya noticed they wore colorful clothes adorned with beads and woven patterns that seemed to shimmer in the sunlight.

"Welcome to the River of Kindness!" said one of the children, a boy with twinkling eyes and a cheerful grin. "I'm Lian, and these are my friends. We're getting water for our village's celebration today."

Maya smiled and introduced herself, feeling instantly at ease. "What's the celebration for?" she asked, intrigued.

Lian's grin widened. "It's a day to honor the river," he said. "Every year, the river brings life to our villages. It's our source of water, food, and connection. The river flows through many villages along its way, and each one celebrates in its own way. But today is special—today, we come together."

As they chatted, Maya learned that the river connected a long string of villages, each with its unique customs and traditions, yet bound by their shared dependence on the river. The villagers saw the river as a friend, a gift that belonged to all of them, uniting them in a web of kindness and cooperation.

As Maya helped fill water jars, a young girl named Nia told her about a tradition where each villager gave a small token of kindness to someone from another village. "It doesn't have to be anything big," Nia explained as she handed Maya a woven bracelet. "Sometimes, it's a song, a small piece of fruit, or even a story. Today, our village is preparing gifts for our neighbors downstream. We want them to feel our gratitude and joy."

Maya's heart swelled with admiration. The idea of sharing simple, heartfelt gifts with strangers was beautiful. She decided she wanted to be a part of this and asked if she could help prepare the gifts. Nia's eyes sparkled with excitement, and together they made their way to a small clearing where villagers were gathering their offerings.

In the clearing, woven baskets were filled with an array of simple yet lovely gifts. There were bundles of fragrant herbs, little clay figurines, and even a few freshly baked bread loaves. Maya could feel the love and care that went into each gift. Nearby, a group of villagers was practicing a song they planned to sing to the next village. Their voices blended in harmony, their melodies carrying the spirit of kindness and unity.

After working alongside the villagers for a while, Maya noticed an elderly woman sitting alone on a woven mat, looking troubled. Her hair was silver, and her face was kind yet creased with worry. Maya hesitated for a moment, then walked over to her.

"Hello," Maya said gently. "Is everything okay?"

The woman looked up, her eyes softening as she took in Maya's warm expression. "Ah, child, you are kind to ask. My name is Esi," she said, managing a small smile. "I was planning to visit my sister in the village across the river, but my legs are not what they used to be, and I fear the journey might be too hard for me today."

Maya felt a wave of compassion. "I can help you get there if you'd like," she offered without hesitation. Esi's face brightened, and with a grateful nod, she accepted. Together, they walked slowly toward the riverbank, where small wooden boats bobbed gently, ready to ferry people across.

The boat ride was peaceful, with the rhythmic sound of water lapping against the boat's side. As they glided down the river, Esi began to tell Maya stories of her youth. She spoke of the times when the river would rise and flow through the villages, bringing people together to help one another rebuild. She described how, in times of scarcity, one village would share its food with the others, and how, during festivals, everyone would come together to celebrate as if they were one big family. Her stories painted a picture of unity and generosity, woven into the lives of everyone who lived along the river.

When they reached the opposite bank, Esi's sister greeted them warmly, her face lighting up at the sight of her sister. Maya watched as the sisters embraced, their happiness a reminder of the power of simple acts of kindness. After exchanging gifts and stories, Maya felt her heart swell with joy, knowing that she had been able to help.

Chapter 3: The Tree of Many Colors

As rain clouds drifted away and the sun broke through, Maya found herself irresistibly drawn back to *The Book of Endless Stories*. She gently flipped through its thick, weathered pages, wondering what new adventure awaited her. A soft illustration caught her eye: a massive, ancient tree with branches reaching wide, each leaf a different color, gleaming like tiny jewels in the sunlight. Curious, she leaned closer, and before she could blink, she was there, standing at the foot of the enormous tree.

The tree was even grander up close. It towered above her, with thick roots stretching deep into the earth, and branches so vast they seemed to reach into the sky. Each leaf sparkled in a hue more brilliant than the last. Maya marveled at the sight; she had never seen anything like it. As she stepped closer, her gaze landed on a small sign carved into one of the roots, reading, "The Tree of Many Colors."

Suddenly, she heard a gentle rustling from above, and a voice, warm and ancient, spoke softly, "Welcome, Maya."

Startled, Maya looked around but saw no one. The voice continued, "I am the Tree of Many Colors. I have grown here for centuries, witnessing countless lives, each leaf representing a different quality or virtue."

Maya felt a sense of awe wash over her. She had heard of trees that bore fruits, flowers, or even songs in some stories, but a tree that held qualities—this was something entirely new. She looked up and saw the colors glimmering in shades of courage, wisdom, empathy, joy, and kindness, among others.

"You are welcome to explore the branches," the Tree said. "Each one is unique, but together they form the whole of who we are."

Maya nodded, feeling a thrill of curiosity and wonder. She reached out to touch the lowest branch, a vibrant green hue that felt warm and inviting under her fingers. The moment she touched it, a scene unfolded before her eyes. She was no longer standing by the tree but in a village, surrounded by people bustling about their daily lives.

She watched a young woman helping an elderly neighbor carry a heavy basket. Children played nearby, and when one of them fell, the others quickly gathered to check on him, offering comfort and a small flower to cheer him up. Maya realized that this green branch held the quality of compassion. Here, people cared for one another, ensuring that no one felt alone or forgotten.

A deep feeling of warmth filled her as she observed these simple acts of kindness. They weren't grand gestures, but each small act seemed to brighten the day for someone else. She wanted to take this warmth with her and wondered if, somehow, she already had.

Returning to the tree, she moved along its branches, her fingers brushing against each one in turn. Each time she touched a different branch, a new scene unfolded before her.

When she touched a bright blue branch, she found herself in a bustling marketplace. She noticed that each person treated the other with deep respect, whether they were buying, selling, or simply passing by. Merchants offered fair prices, and shoppers showed gratitude. People listened carefully to each other, valuing every word spoken. Here, she realized, was the branch of respect. The marketplace was lively, filled with chatter and laughter, yet it was peaceful, each person aware of the importance of honoring those around them.

As she let go of the blue branch, Maya felt her heart grow a little wider. She understood now that respect wasn't just about words but about truly valuing each person, each interaction. Moving along, she came to a branch of warm golden light, glowing as if it held the sun's rays within.

Touching the golden branch brought her to a new scene, a place where people worked together, building homes, gardens, and roads for their community. She saw individuals of all ages lending a hand, each contributing in their own way. This branch embodied teamwork and unity. No one was left out, and each person's unique skills added to the strength of the group. Maya watched as a group of people worked side by side, laughing and sharing stories as they built a bridge. She sensed the beauty of working together and knew this lesson would stay with her.

Eagerly, she continued exploring the branches. Each branch opened a new world and a new lesson. She touched a silver branch and found herself in a place where people valued honesty. Here, everyone's words were trusted because they spoke with truth and integrity. She learned how powerful honesty could be, how it strengthened relationships and built a foundation of trust. Maya smiled as she watched children playing, sharing secrets without fear because they trusted each other completely.

Maya returned to the tree, and now she felt something shifting within her. She sensed the qualities she had witnessed blending into her own being. She felt a new courage, a deeper respect for others, and a desire to act with compassion and honesty. The Tree of Many Colors seemed to be showing her that each quality, while valuable on its own, became even more powerful when it was part of something greater.

The next branch she reached for shimmered with an iridescent purple, and Maya felt a calmness wash over her as she touched it. This branch led her to a world where people cherished silence, using it to reflect and listen. Here, she learned that sometimes the greatest respect was found in quiet moments, in listening rather than speaking. She observed people sitting together without words, yet their bond was profound, strengthened by their silent understanding. It was a new kind of strength, one that came from within.

The Tree's wisdom seemed endless, each branch revealing another layer of the world's beauty, all connected yet unique. As she explored further, she came across a crimson branch that radiated with warmth and fire. Here, she encountered bravery. She saw people facing challenges with courage and resilience. Some faced difficult choices, others dealt with fears or adversities, yet all acted with a brave heart. Maya felt a stirring in her chest, a reminder that bravery wasn't just for heroes in stories but for everyone willing to stand up for what they believed in.

Chapter 4: The Whispering Forest

Maya's mind was buzzing with the wisdom she had gained from the Tree of Many Colors. She felt richer for the journey, as though the colors and qualities she had encountered were now woven into her very being. She could hardly wait to see what *The Book of Endless Stories* would show her next. With a quiet thrill, she opened the book once more. Her fingers brushed a page that held an intricate drawing of a dense, shadowy forest filled with tall, mysterious trees. Each tree seemed to have faces carved into its bark, and the branches stretched out like arms extending to welcome her. She leaned in closer, and in the blink of an eye, she found herself standing at the edge of the forest.

The trees loomed tall and mighty, their bark rough and aged, each one holding a story of its own. Mist swirled around her feet, and the air was filled with the scent of moss and earth. The silence here was different—it felt alive, thick with a quiet power, as though the trees were holding secrets from long ago. Maya stood still, captivated by the mysterious atmosphere. Suddenly, she heard a faint whisper, soft and melodic, like a song carried on a gentle breeze. She glanced around, but saw no one. The whispering seemed to come from the trees themselves, as if they were speaking to each other.

"Hello?" Maya called out softly, half-expecting the trees to answer her.

To her surprise, the whispering grew louder, and a voice, deep and resonant, spoke from a tree nearby. "Welcome, Maya," it said, the voice calm and warm. "I am Thal, an elder of the Whispering Forest. You have entered a place of stories."

Maya was intrigued. She moved closer to the tree that had spoken, its bark gnarled and dark, with patterns that looked like eyes and lips frozen in ancient expressions. "A place of stories?" she repeated, curiosity sparking in her eyes.

"Yes," Thal replied. "This forest holds the memories and voices of those who came before. Each tree here has a tale to tell, a piece of wisdom to share. The whispering you hear is the sound of these stories, spoken softly so that only those who truly listen can hear."

Maya's heart quickened with excitement. She had always loved stories, and to be in a forest filled with them was a dream come true. She closed her eyes for a moment, focusing on the soft murmurs around her. The trees spoke in different voices, some deep and rumbling, others soft and gentle, all mingling together in a melody of whispered words.

"May I hear one of these stories?" she asked, her voice filled with wonder.

"Of course," Thal said, his voice almost a chuckle. "But remember, child, listening is an art. To truly hear, you must open not only your ears but also your heart. Will you listen, Maya?"

She nodded eagerly, settling herself on a patch of soft moss at the base of Thal's trunk. She closed her eyes again, letting the whispers surround her, each word weaving into the next, creating a tapestry of voices that spanned ages. Slowly, one voice rose above the others, steady and clear, and a story began to unfold.

She saw an image in her mind: a young girl named Lira living in a small, quiet village. Lira was known for her curiosity and her eagerness to explore, but she had one quality that set her apart—she was a remarkable listener. Lira would sit for hours by the village well, listening to the elders talk about their lives, their struggles, and the lessons they had learned. She never interrupted, never questioned; she simply listened, absorbing each story as if it were a precious gift.

One day, Lira noticed a stranger visiting the village, a wanderer who looked weary and lost. Without hesitation, she approached him and invited him to sit by the well. He looked surprised but accepted her invitation. She listened as he told her about his long journey, the challenges he had faced, and the loved ones he missed. He spoke of his worries, his hopes, and his regrets. When he finished, he looked at her, expecting advice or answers. But Lira simply smiled, her eyes filled with understanding, and thanked him for sharing his story. The wanderer left the village that day with a lighter heart, his burdens eased by the simple act of being heard.

As Maya listened to this story, she felt a deep understanding blossom within her. She had never realized the power of listening in such a way. She opened her eyes and looked up at Thal, gratitude shining in her gaze.

"Thank you," she whispered. "I never knew that listening could be so powerful."

Thal's branches rustled, as though he were nodding. "Listening is a gift, Maya. It is one of the most precious forms of kindness you can offer. In truly listening, you give others the space to be themselves, to share their joys and sorrows, without judgment or interruption."

Maya absorbed Thal's words, feeling the weight of their meaning settle into her heart. She glanced around the forest, her senses attuned to the other voices whispering through the trees. Each voice held its own story, its own truth. She wanted to hear them all, to learn from each one. She moved slowly through the forest, placing her hand on each tree she passed. With each touch, a new story began to unfold.

Chapter 5: The Sky of Dreams

Maya felt the urge to open *The Book of Endless Stories* again, her heart beating with anticipation for whatever adventure awaited her next. The book was quickly becoming more than just a collection of tales—it was a portal into realms that felt both familiar and fantastical, each one weaving its own lessons into the fabric of her understanding. This time, as she opened the book, her gaze fell upon an illustration of a vast, star-filled sky. Its deep, endless blue was dotted with stars that twinkled brightly, arranged in constellations she'd never seen before. Some stars were larger than others, some shone with unusual colors, and some even seemed to form patterns and images that beckoned her to come closer. Before she knew it, she was surrounded by that very sky.

Maya found herself floating in a quiet, dreamlike realm, surrounded by stars that twinkled like diamonds scattered across an endless dark-blue canvas. The air felt different here—lighter, almost like the sky itself was alive, pulsing with magic. Maya marveled at the beauty surrounding her. She felt as though she was soaring through a dream, and every breath she took filled her with wonder. She looked around, captivated by the constellations, which seemed to glow with an inner light.

Suddenly, one of the stars grew brighter, and a voice echoed softly from it. "Welcome, Maya."

Startled but curious, she turned to face the star that had spoken. It shimmered in soft colors, shifting between shades of silver, blue, and lavender. The voice was gentle, almost musical, and it wrapped around her like a comforting breeze.

"Who are you?" Maya asked, her voice filled with awe.

"I am Solara," the star replied. "This is the Sky of Dreams, where the dreams of many hearts are woven into constellations. Each star represents a dream, a wish, or a hope that someone, somewhere, holds dear. Some are young and newly formed, others have shone for centuries. Together, they create a tapestry of dreams, showing the world's infinite possibilities."

Maya felt a thrill of excitement. She had always loved dreaming and thinking about what could be, and now she was in a place where dreams were alive, lighting up the sky itself. She took a deep breath, gazing at the stars surrounding her, each one twinkling with its own story. She wondered how many dreams were out there, floating through this endless expanse, each one special in its own way.

"Can I... see some of these dreams?" she asked Solara, her heart pounding with curiosity.

"Yes," Solara said, her voice filled with warmth. "But remember, Maya, each dream is unique. Some are simple, some are grand, some are joyful, and some are bittersweet. Each one, no matter its shape or size, carries its own beauty."

Maya nodded, feeling both excitement and a quiet respect for the dreams that lay before her. She reached out to the closest star, a small golden one that shimmered softly. The moment she touched it, an image appeared, filling the sky around her with vibrant colors.

She saw a little boy tending to a garden filled with flowers. He knelt beside each plant, carefully watering and nurturing it with a tender touch. Maya could see that he cared deeply for every blossom, hoping they would grow tall and beautiful. His dream was simple: he wished to see his flowers bloom. The vision was humble, yet Maya felt its warmth. She realized that even the smallest dreams could bring beauty into the world. As she let go of the star, the image faded, but its peaceful energy remained with her.

Maya reached out to another star, this one a cool, shimmering blue. When she touched it, she was swept into the dream of a young girl who longed to travel beyond her home village, to see what lay beyond the mountains she had always known. The girl's eyes sparkled with wonder as she imagined herself exploring distant lands, discovering new sights, and meeting new friends. Her dream was one of adventure and courage, and Maya felt herself inspired by the girl's yearning to explore and learn about the world.

Letting go of the blue star, Maya turned her gaze to a larger, brighter one that shone with a fierce, warm glow. As she touched it, a new vision appeared before her. She saw an older man who, despite his years, was still filled with energy and passion. His dream was to teach, to pass on his knowledge to others so that they could carry forward the wisdom he had spent a lifetime gathering. Maya watched as he patiently guided children through lessons, his eyes lighting up whenever one of them understood a new concept. His dream wasn't for himself, but for others, and Maya felt a deep respect for the man's dedication and generosity.

She moved through the sky, touching star after star, each one revealing a new dream. One dream showed her a woman who wished for peace in her community, her heart heavy with love and hope as she watched over her family and neighbors. Another star showed a young child who dreamed of growing strong, hoping to help their parents with the family farm one day. Each dream was different, yet each one glowed with its own unique light, filling the sky with a tapestry of hopes and aspirations.

As Maya continued, she noticed a small, faint star off to one side. Its light was dim, barely noticeable among the other brilliant stars. Curious, she reached out to it, wondering why its light was so soft. The vision that appeared was of a young girl who wished to speak confidently in front of her class. She dreamed of one day standing up and sharing her ideas without fear, her heart full of the desire to be heard and valued. Maya felt a pang of empathy; the girl's dream was so gentle, so quiet, yet it held a strength that touched Maya's heart. She whispered a wish for the girl, hoping that one day her voice would shine as brightly as any other.

Moving on, Maya found a star that was constantly shifting in color, flickering between shades of green, purple, and gold. When she touched it, she saw a person with a dream to protect the forests, rivers, and creatures of the earth. This dream was fierce and vibrant, filled with a determination that felt like a powerful heartbeat. Maya could sense the love the person had for the world around them, a love so strong that it fueled their desire to make a difference. She felt inspired by their resolve and promised herself that she, too, would cherish and protect the beauty of the world.

Eventually, she came upon a massive star that glowed with a steady, brilliant light. Its warmth seemed to wrap around her, and as she touched it, the vision that unfolded was unlike any she had seen before. This was the dream of a person who wished to bring people together, to create a world where everyone, regardless of who they were, felt safe and accepted. Maya watched as this dreamer worked tirelessly to build bridges of understanding, teaching others the value of compassion and unity. It was a dream for the world, a vision of harmony, and Maya felt humbled by the dreamer's boundless hope.

Chapter 6: The Garden of Forgotten Voices

On a quiet afternoon, Maya settled once again into her favorite corner with *The Book of Endless Stories* resting on her lap. Each journey she'd taken through the book had filled her with new understanding, new emotions, and new perspectives. Today, as she flipped open to a page near the center, she saw an image of a lush, green garden bursting with flowers in every color imaginable. The flowers seemed to move as if alive, their petals waving in a breeze she could almost feel. Without a moment's hesitation, she closed her eyes, and when she opened them, she was standing in that very garden.

The air was filled with a sweet fragrance, a blend of flowers and fresh earth, and a gentle wind caressed her face. Maya looked around, taking in the vibrant blossoms that grew in abundance around her. Each flower seemed unique—some were tall and regal, while others were small and delicate, but all were equally beautiful. The colors were vivid, ranging from fiery reds and oranges to cool blues and purples, with shades she had never even imagined. She felt like she had stepped into a place filled with magic.

She took a few steps forward, marveling at the variety of flowers, when she heard a soft voice, like a whisper carried on the wind. "Welcome, Maya."

Startled, Maya turned to see an elderly woman tending to the flowers nearby. The woman's hair was silver and fell in soft waves over her shoulders. Her face was gentle, her expression warm, and her hands moved gracefully as she touched each flower with the kind of care that made it seem as if she was greeting an old friend.

"Hello," Maya replied, intrigued. "Is this your garden?"

The woman smiled, her eyes twinkling. "Yes, you could say that. My name is Yara, and I am the keeper of the Garden of Forgotten Voices."

Maya felt a shiver of curiosity. "Forgotten voices?"

Yara nodded, her gaze softening as she looked out over the garden. "Each flower here represents a voice that has been overlooked, unheard, or forgotten. These are the voices of people who, for one reason or another, have been silenced or ignored. I care for them, nurturing each one so it can bloom, even if no one else is listening."

Maya's heart swelled with compassion. She looked around at the thousands of flowers, wondering about the stories they held. She imagined the people whose voices had grown quiet, whose words had drifted away without ever being truly heard. The thought made her feel a deep sadness, but also a fierce desire to know more.

Yara gestured to a delicate white flower nearby, its petals shimmering faintly. "Would you like to hear one of their stories?" she asked.

Maya nodded, kneeling beside the flower. She closed her eyes, allowing herself to focus fully on the gentle hum of the garden around her. Slowly, she felt a story begin to unfold in her mind, a voice rising softly, as if someone was speaking to her from far away.

She saw the image of a young girl, sitting alone on the edge of a playground, watching the other children play. The girl longed to join them, but each time she tried to speak, her voice came out in a whisper, too quiet to be heard. She was shy and afraid, worried that her words wouldn't matter to anyone else. And so, she remained silent, her heart aching with the desire to connect, to be a part of the laughter and joy around her. But day after day, she remained invisible, her voice lost in the noise of the world around her.

Maya felt a pang in her chest as the story faded, leaving her with a sense of the girl's quiet loneliness. She opened her eyes and looked up at Yara. "Is there anything we can do to help her?" she asked, her voice filled with concern.

Yara gave a gentle nod. "Sometimes, all it takes is someone who is willing to listen, someone who makes space for others' voices. When you truly listen to someone, it gives their words weight, their presence meaning."

Maya looked around the garden with new eyes, seeing each flower as a person, a life, a story waiting to be heard. She reached out to a nearby blue flower, letting its story fill her mind.

This time, she saw an older woman working hard every day to support her family, her hands rough and calloused from years of labor. She rarely spoke of her struggles or her dreams, focusing instead on ensuring that her children had what they needed. She had stories of her own—memories of her youth, of the places she had been, of the dreams she had set aside. But no one asked her about these things, so her stories remained buried, forgotten, while she continued to work in silence.

Maya felt a wave of gratitude for the woman's sacrifices, and a sadness that no one had ever listened to her. She turned to Yara, her voice thoughtful. "Every one of these flowers has a story like that, don't they?"

Yara nodded. "Yes. Each one represents someone who has felt unseen, someone whose voice has drifted into silence. But they all bloom here, reminding us that every voice matters, even if it isn't always heard."

Maya took a deep breath, letting the stories settle in her heart. She reached for a yellow flower nearby, wanting to hear more, and closed her eyes as another voice rose.

She saw a boy who had always dreamed of becoming an artist. He would draw whenever he could, creating pictures of the world as he saw it, filled with colors and shapes that made sense to him. But his family, his friends, even his teachers, didn't understand his art. They told him to focus on practical things, to keep his head out of the clouds. Gradually, he stopped drawing, his dreams fading as he grew up. His art, his voice, became another whisper lost in the crowd.

Maya's heart ached for the boy. She understood now that there were so many people whose voices were lost, whose stories went unheard simply because no one had taken the time to listen. She felt a deep longing to remember each voice, to hold space for them so they would not be forgotten.

Chapter 7: The Bridge of Understanding

As Maya returned to *The Book of Endless Stories,* she found herself feeling more excited than ever. Each adventure had opened her eyes to new worlds and new ways of seeing others, and the lessons she was learning felt like gifts she could carry forever. Today, as she opened the book, she saw an illustration of a long, winding bridge that spanned a deep, misty gorge. The bridge was made of thick, intertwined vines and sturdy wooden planks, with bright, colorful flowers blooming along its sides. She felt the familiar tug of magic, and before she knew it, she was standing at the edge of that bridge.

The air was crisp and cool, filled with the scent of wildflowers. She looked around, noting that the bridge connected two hillsides, each one shrouded in mist and mystery. As she took a step forward, the bridge creaked slightly beneath her feet, but it held firm. She felt a sense of wonder as she gazed out at the swirling mists below, wondering where the bridge might lead.

"Welcome, Maya," a voice called out, breaking the silence. She turned and saw a figure standing on the other end of the bridge, waving to her. It was a tall man with a calm, thoughtful expression, dressed in robes that seemed to shimmer with every color of the rainbow. His eyes held a kind, wise look, and his presence radiated warmth.

Maya took a few cautious steps closer, and the man smiled. "My name is Kavi, and I am the Keeper of the Bridge of Understanding," he said, his voice gentle yet firm. "This bridge connects worlds, people, and ideas. It is a place where differences can meet, and where understanding can be found."

Maya felt a thrill of curiosity. "What do you mean by understanding?" she asked, gazing down the length of the bridge.

Kavi's smile widened. "Understanding is when we make space for others' views, feelings, and experiences. It's when we open our hearts to truly see someone else's perspective, even if it's different from our own. The bridge helps people find common ground."

Maya nodded slowly, absorbing his words. She had always believed in the importance of kindness and empathy, but this idea of understanding felt deeper, as if it were a bridge that connected hearts and minds.

"Would you like to cross the bridge, Maya?" Kavi asked, his eyes twinkling. "On the way, you'll meet others with stories to share. Each one has their own view, their own experiences. If you listen with an open heart, you may find that, though their journeys are different from yours, there is wisdom to be found."

Maya nodded, feeling ready. She began walking, her footsteps soft on the wooden planks. As she reached the middle of the bridge, she saw two people standing near each other, though they were facing in opposite directions and seemed unwilling to look at one another. They appeared to be in the midst of an argument, each one gesturing passionately.

The first person, a young woman named Liana, was speaking in a tense, frustrated tone. "You never listen to me," she said, looking away from the man beside her. "You're so focused on your own plans that you never consider how I feel."

The man, who introduced himself as Joren, replied just as tensely, "And you're always so cautious, so afraid to take risks. I have dreams too, but you don't seem to care."

Maya watched them both, feeling the frustration and hurt in their voices. She could see how each person was holding onto their own viewpoint, so focused on their feelings that they couldn't see the other's. She thought back to the lessons she had learned in the Whispering Forest about listening, and took a deep breath.

"Excuse me," she said gently, stepping closer. "Maybe if you tried to see things from each other's point of view, it would help you understand each other."

Liana and Joren glanced at her, surprised. They looked at each other hesitantly, and Maya encouraged them to take a step back and listen without interrupting. As each of them shared their thoughts, Maya saw a shift in their expressions. Liana softened as she heard Joren talk about his dreams, and Joren grew thoughtful as Liana explained her concerns.

Maya felt a warmth bloom in her chest as she watched them begin to understand each other, realizing that both of their views had value. She thanked them, feeling grateful for the lesson they had taught her about seeing beyond her own perspective. She continued her journey across the bridge, feeling the magic of understanding settling into her heart.

As she walked further, she came across a boy and a girl sitting on the bridge, both looking upset. When she approached, they introduced themselves as Theo and Amara. They were siblings who had been in a disagreement about how to spend their free time. Theo wanted to explore and play games, while Amara preferred reading and drawing. Their voices were tense as they argued, each one convinced that their way of spending time was better.

Maya knelt down beside them, a gentle smile on her face. "You know, sometimes understanding means finding a balance," she suggested. "Maybe you could each take turns, so you get to try both activities."

Theo and Amara exchanged glances, their expressions softening. Slowly, they agreed to take turns, with Theo promising to spend time with Amara doing her favorite activities if she would do the same for him. They thanked Maya, and she felt a deep satisfaction watching them come to a peaceful solution. She realized that understanding didn't always mean changing who you were; sometimes it was about compromise and finding a middle ground.

Chapter 8: The Mountain of Courage

It was a chilly morning when Maya sat down with *The Book of Endless Stories,* eager to see where it would take her this time. She took a deep breath, opened to a new page, and saw an illustration of a mountain rising tall and proud against a misty sky. The mountain's peak was shrouded in clouds, giving it an air of mystery and challenge. Something about it stirred Maya's heart, filling her with a quiet thrill and a hint of apprehension. Before she knew it, she felt the familiar pull of magic, and when she opened her eyes, she was standing at the base of that very mountain.

The air was cool and crisp, filled with the scent of pine and the earthy smell of rock and soil. She could feel the towering presence of the mountain above her, stretching so high that she couldn't see the summit. The path leading upward was narrow and steep, winding through dense forests and rocky outcroppings. Maya felt a mix of excitement and nervousness. She had never climbed a mountain before, and the task seemed daunting.

"Welcome, Maya," a deep voice called out. She looked around and saw a tall, strong figure standing a few steps ahead on the path. He was an older man, his face weathered and wise, with eyes that sparkled like the mountain streams she could hear rushing in the distance. He wore simple, sturdy clothes and carried a staff carved from a dark, polished wood.

"My name is Dara," he said with a warm smile. "I am the guide of the Mountain of Courage. Many have come to this mountain seeking strength, resilience, and the courage to face their fears."

Maya felt a spark of determination rise within her. "I want to climb it," she said, her voice filled with conviction. "I want to learn what courage really means."

Dara nodded approvingly. "Courage comes in many forms, Maya. It is not just about facing physical dangers, but also about standing strong in the face of doubt, fear, and challenges from within. As you climb, you'll encounter trials that may seem difficult or even impossible, but remember, courage is a journey of the heart as much as it is a journey of the body."

With that, he gestured for her to follow him, and together they began the ascent. The path was steep and rocky, and soon Maya felt her legs straining as they climbed higher. But as they walked, she kept her focus on each step, determined to keep going.

After a short while, they reached a plateau, where Dara stopped and pointed to a small cave nearby. "Inside this cave is the first trial," he said, his voice gentle but firm. "It's known as the Cave of Doubts. You may find that things are not as they seem, and your own doubts may appear before you, challenging you to face them."

Maya hesitated, feeling a knot of uncertainty in her stomach, but she nodded and walked toward the cave. The entrance was dark and foreboding, with shadows flickering along the walls as she stepped inside. As her eyes adjusted to the dim light, she noticed shapes moving around her, whispering words that sent shivers down her spine.

"Are you sure you're strong enough for this journey?" a voice murmured from the shadows. "What if you fail? What if you're not brave enough?" Maya could feel her confidence waver as these words sank in. Doubts she had never acknowledged began to surface, making her feel small and uncertain.

She took a deep breath, reminding herself of Dara's words. "Courage is facing doubt and pushing through it," she whispered to herself, steadying her resolve. She continued walking through the cave, confronting each whisper of doubt with her own quiet strength. The shadows seemed to grow quieter, and as she neared the exit, she felt lighter, as though a weight had lifted from her shoulders.

When she stepped out of the cave, Dara was waiting for her, a proud smile on his face. "Well done, Maya," he said. "You have faced your doubts and continued forward. That is the first step of courage."

They resumed their climb, and soon the path grew steeper and more treacherous. Maya's legs began to ache, and her breath came in gasps, but she kept going, determined to reach the top. As they climbed higher, Dara pointed to a cliffside where a narrow ledge jutted out over a deep ravine. "The second trial awaits," he said. "It's called the Ledge of Uncertainty. You'll need to cross it to continue on your journey."

Maya looked at the ledge, her heart pounding. The drop below was dizzying, and the ledge was barely wide enough for her feet. Her hands trembled as she took a cautious step forward, her eyes fixed on the narrow path. She could feel her fear building with each step, her mind racing with worries of what could happen if she slipped.

But as she took another step, she remembered Dara's words about courage. It wasn't about ignoring her fear, but about moving forward despite it. She focused on each step, steadying her breath and calming her mind. With each careful movement, her fear lessened, replaced by a growing sense of strength. When she finally reached the other side, she felt a surge of pride. She had faced her fear and made it through.

Dara joined her with an encouraging nod. "You have crossed the Ledge of Uncertainty, Maya. Each step you took was a step of courage, moving forward even when fear tried to hold you back."

They continued up the mountain, climbing through thick forests and over rocky terrain. As they went higher, Maya noticed that the air grew colder, the path rougher. Eventually, they reached a small clearing where a roaring wind whipped through the trees, pulling at her clothes and hair. Dara gestured to a tree at the edge of the clearing, where a small pouch hung from a branch, swaying in the fierce wind.

"This is the Test of Resilience," Dara explained. "The wind represents the obstacles life throws at us. To pass this test, you must reach the pouch without letting the wind push you back."

Maya squared her shoulders, bracing herself as she walked toward the tree. The wind was relentless, battering her from all sides, and each step was a struggle. She felt her energy fading as the wind pushed against her, trying to force her back. But she planted her feet firmly, refusing to give up. With every step, she reminded herself of her strength, of her determination to reach the pouch.

Chapter 9: The Circle of Trust

The field was beautiful, filled with wildflowers in every shade of blue, yellow, and purple, and the air was warm, carrying the scent of freshly cut grass. In the middle of the field stood a group of people, all arranged in a wide, unbroken circle. Each one seemed to glow with a quiet strength and warmth that Maya could feel even from a distance. She felt drawn to them, as if something was pulling her into their midst.

As she approached, a gentle voice called out, "Welcome, Maya."

Turning, she saw an elderly woman standing just outside the circle. Her hair was silver, her eyes warm and kind, and she wore a simple, flowing robe that seemed to catch the light. Her expression was calm, with a hint of wisdom that made Maya feel immediately at ease.

"My name is Amina," the woman said, smiling. "I am the Keeper of the Circle of Trust. Here, people from different walks of life come together, each bringing their own strengths and vulnerabilities, forming a bond built on trust."

Maya was intrigued. She had always thought of trust as something shared between friends and family, but as she looked at the circle, she could tell that this was something different. Each person seemed focused on the others, connected by more than just proximity. She could feel the unity that flowed between them, as if their trust was woven together into an invisible yet unbreakable thread.

"What do you mean by the Circle of Trust?" Maya asked, curious.

Amina gestured for her to step closer, and Maya moved to stand beside her at the edge of the circle. "Trust, Maya, is not only about knowing someone well or having history with them. It's about sharing parts of yourself and opening yourself to others, without the fear of judgment or betrayal. In this circle, people trust one another fully, knowing that they are safe to be who they truly are."

Maya nodded slowly, trying to absorb her words. She watched as people in the circle exchanged smiles and soft words, and she felt a warm energy radiating from them, as if each person's presence strengthened the circle. She realized that trust wasn't just something you gave; it was something you shared, something that grew with each person's contribution.

Amina reached out and took her hand gently. "Would you like to join the circle, Maya?" she asked, her voice inviting.

Maya felt a surge of excitement mixed with a hint of nervousness, but she nodded, letting Amina lead her to an open spot in the circle. As she stood there, holding the hands of the people on either side of her, she felt a new sensation, a warmth that seemed to flow through her, connecting her to each person in the circle. It was as if trust itself had become something tangible, a force that moved from one hand to the next, growing stronger with each connection.

Amina stepped into the center of the circle and spoke to everyone gathered. "Today, we are here to strengthen the bonds of trust. Each of us comes with our own hopes, fears, and stories, and by sharing them, we weave them into the fabric of our circle."

One by one, people began to speak, sharing their stories, their worries, their dreams. Maya listened intently, feeling both the courage it took for each person to open up and the kindness with which the others received them. She heard a young woman speak about her fear of failure, a father express his hopes for his children, an elderly man talk about the loneliness he sometimes felt, and a young boy share his dream of becoming a storyteller.

With each story shared, the circle seemed to grow warmer and stronger, as if every word spoken added another thread to the fabric of trust that bound them all. Maya felt inspired by the honesty and vulnerability of each person, and she realized that trust was built not only on promises or shared experiences but on the willingness to be open and real with one another.

When it was Maya's turn to speak, she felt a moment of hesitation, but then she looked around at the faces surrounding her, each one filled with encouragement and understanding. She took a deep breath and began to speak about her own fears, her own hopes, and the journey she was on, learning about kindness, courage, and understanding through her adventures in the book. She shared her wish to carry these lessons with her, to make a difference in the lives of those she met.

As she spoke, she felt the warmth of the circle flow into her, reassuring her, lifting her, and she knew that she was accepted, flaws and all. It was a powerful feeling, one that she knew she would carry with her always.

After she finished, the person beside her gave her hand a gentle squeeze, a silent message of support. She looked around the circle and felt a deep sense of belonging, a connection that went beyond words. Trust, she realized, wasn't just about putting faith in others; it was about opening herself up, sharing her true self, and being willing to accept others as they were.

Chapter 10: The Dance of Respect

On a quiet evening, the golden glow of twilight filling her room, Maya once again opened *The Book of Endless Stories*. She had come to love the magical journeys it took her on, each one teaching her something about herself and the world around her. She felt the excitement bubbling within her as her fingers turned to a new page. This time, she found herself looking at a painting of a village filled with people, each one in motion, their movements graceful and rhythmic, as if they were part of a dance. She felt herself being drawn in, the familiar sensation of magic swirling around her, and when she opened her eyes, she was standing in the heart of that very village.

The village was alive with energy, filled with people moving in a beautiful harmony. Men, women, and children danced through the streets, their steps light and purposeful. Each person moved differently, expressing something unique, yet together they created a pattern that felt both gentle and powerful, like a river flowing in unison toward the same destination. Maya watched, mesmerized, as the villagers danced with a quiet joy, their faces serene and focused. She had never seen anything like it before.

"Welcome, Maya," a voice called out gently, drawing her attention. She turned to see a young woman approaching her, her movements as graceful as those of the dancers around her. She wore a flowing dress adorned with small, colorful beads that shimmered as she moved. Her smile was warm, and her eyes held a kindness that made Maya feel instantly at ease.

"My name is Alani," the woman said, inclining her head in greeting. "I am one of the keepers of the Dance of Respect. Here, we celebrate the beauty of individuality, harmony, and respect through movement and silence."

Maya felt her curiosity spark. "What do you mean by respect through dance?" she asked, her voice filled with wonder.

Alani's smile grew as she took Maya's hand, leading her gently toward the center of the village. "In our village, we believe that respect is not only something we say or feel, but something we show. Each of us moves in our own way, expressing who we are. Through this dance, we respect each other's space, rhythm, and expression. It is a way of honoring everyone's uniqueness, while finding harmony as a community."

Maya felt a tingle of excitement. She watched as people moved around her, each one expressing themselves through graceful steps, gestures, and expressions. She could see how each dancer moved with an awareness of the people around them, careful not to invade each other's space, respecting each other's rhythm and pace. It was a dance not just of movement, but of understanding and mutual appreciation.

Alani released Maya's hand and gestured toward a group of children nearby, each one practicing small, deliberate steps. They danced in a circle, laughing as they learned to follow the rhythm. "Would you like to join them?" Alani asked.

Maya felt a flutter of nervousness but nodded, drawn to the idea of being part of this harmonious expression. She stepped into the circle, and one of the children, a boy with a wide smile, reached out to hold her hand. The children welcomed her with warmth, and Maya felt her nerves settle as they began teaching her simple steps, laughing and encouraging her when she stumbled.

As she danced, she started to understand that this was more than just movement. The children showed her how to stay aware of those around her, to adjust her steps if someone needed more space, and to respect their pace if they moved slower or faster. It was like a silent language of understanding, each person moving in a way that honored the presence of others. The dance felt both freeing and grounding, and Maya felt a sense of unity with everyone around her.

After a while, Alani called Maya over to another part of the village, where a group of elderly villagers danced with slower, more measured steps. Their movements were filled with grace and wisdom, each one flowing into the next. Maya watched, entranced, as they moved with a deep respect for each other's pace and abilities. She noticed that even though some of the elders moved more slowly, the others adjusted their steps without hesitation, creating a gentle, supportive rhythm that everyone could follow.

Alani leaned in and spoke softly to Maya. "In our dance, we show respect by honoring each person's strengths and limitations. The younger ones learn from the elders, who bring the wisdom of years, while the elders find joy in the energy of the young. Through these movements, respect becomes something we live."

Maya felt a profound admiration for the elders as she watched them dance, each step filled with care and thoughtfulness. She realized that respect wasn't just about giving space to others but also about valuing their unique contributions, seeing the worth in each person's experiences and strengths.

As the evening wore on, Maya followed Alani to another part of the village, where a group of people danced with flowing scarves in vibrant colors. The scarves waved and twisted in the air as the dancers moved, creating a mesmerizing display of color and motion. The dancers moved freely, some faster, some slower, each one creating patterns with their scarves that wove together like a tapestry. Maya noticed that even as they moved individually, they paid close attention to each other's movements, adjusting the flow of their scarves so that they wouldn't interfere with anyone else's dance.

Alani smiled as she watched Maya take it all in. "This part of our dance represents how we respect each other's dreams, beliefs, and aspirations. Each person brings their own color, their own vision, and together we create something beautiful. We celebrate our differences and see them as part of a whole."

Maya felt a surge of inspiration as she watched the dancers. She understood that their movements, though different, formed a harmony that could only exist because each person brought their unique self to the dance. It was a reminder that everyone's individuality was valuable, that respect meant appreciating these differences and creating a space where everyone could shine.

As night began to fall, lanterns were lit around the village, casting a warm glow over the scene. The villagers gathered together once more, forming a large circle in the center of the village. Alani invited Maya to join them, and as she took her place, she felt a quiet strength in the unity of the circle. Each person stood, still and silent, their presence a testament to the respect they held for one another.

Chapter 11: The Valley of Forgiveness

The air was cool and refreshing, with a gentle breeze that carried the scent of fresh grass and blooming flowers. Maya looked around, feeling a sense of tranquility settle over her. The valley was peaceful, yet she sensed a quiet strength in the landscape around her. The river flowed steadily, glistening under the sun, and as she walked along the bank, she noticed a figure standing beneath the tree's shade.

The figure was an elderly man with kind eyes and a gentle expression. His face held a quiet wisdom, and he radiated a warmth that made Maya feel instantly welcome. He wore simple, earth-toned clothes and leaned slightly on a wooden staff, his eyes filled with a softness that only comes from a life well-lived and deeply felt.

"Welcome, Maya," he said, his voice calm and inviting. "I am Eamon, the keeper of the Valley of Forgiveness."

Maya felt a shiver of curiosity. "Forgiveness?" she asked, her voice filled with wonder. "Is this valley a place for forgiveness?"

Eamon nodded, his gaze sweeping across the valley. "Yes, this valley has been a place where people come to learn about forgiveness, a place where they can find peace in letting go of old hurts. Forgiveness is a gift we give to ourselves and to others. It is a journey of the heart."

Maya's heart swelled with curiosity. She had heard about forgiveness before, but she hadn't thought deeply about what it meant. As she looked around, she saw other people walking through the valley, each one seeming to carry a different weight, some light and others heavy. She sensed that each of them was here to let go of something, to find a sense of freedom from the burdens they had been carrying.

"Would you like to walk with me?" Eamon asked, gesturing toward the path that wound along the riverbank.

Maya nodded, and together they began to walk slowly along the path. Eamon's presence was calming, and as they walked, he shared stories of people who had come to the valley seeking forgiveness. He spoke of those who had been hurt by others and those who had hurt others, of people who had struggled to forgive and those who had been forgiven.

As they walked, they came across a woman sitting by the river, her face filled with sadness. She looked up as Maya and Eamon approached, and Eamon introduced her as Lyra. She greeted Maya with a small, weary smile, and as they sat beside her, she shared her story.

"I was hurt by someone I trusted," she began, her voice trembling slightly. "A friend whom I thought would always stand by me... but they let me down when I needed them the most. I felt betrayed, abandoned. And I carried that hurt with me for so long, feeling that it defined me, that it was part of who I was."

Maya felt a pang of empathy for Lyra. She could see the weight of her pain, the hurt that had lingered in her heart. Lyra continued, her gaze drifting to the river. "But as I sat here, watching the river flow, I began to see things differently. The river doesn't hold onto anything—it flows, letting each moment go, making space for the next. I realized that I had been holding onto my pain, letting it define me, when I could choose to release it."

Eamon smiled softly, his eyes filled with understanding. "Forgiveness is like the river, Lyra. It is not about forgetting, but about releasing, about freeing yourself from the burdens of the past so you can make space for peace."

Maya listened intently, feeling the wisdom in Eamon's words. She could see how forgiveness, like the steady flow of the river, could create a sense of freedom, allowing people to move forward without being weighed down by the hurts of the past.

They continued their walk, and soon they came upon a man who stood gazing out over the valley. His face was lined with regret, his shoulders slightly slumped. Eamon introduced him as Lian, and he welcomed them with a nod. As they stood together, he shared his story, his voice filled with remorse.

"I hurt someone I cared about," Lian began, his eyes filled with a quiet pain. "In a moment of anger, I said things I didn't mean, things that hurt them deeply. I've carried that regret with me, wishing I could take back my words, wishing I could change what I did. But I know that I can't go back."

Eamon placed a reassuring hand on Lian's shoulder. "Regret is a heavy burden, Lian. But forgiveness is not only about seeking forgiveness from others; it is also about forgiving ourselves. To forgive oneself is to acknowledge our mistakes, to take responsibility, but also to find the courage to let go and grow."

Maya felt a surge of understanding as she listened to Lian's story. She realized that forgiveness wasn't just about forgiving others; it was also about finding a way to forgive oneself, to release the guilt and pain that could weigh a person down.

As they continued along the path, Eamon shared more stories, each one revealing a different facet of forgiveness. They met people who had forgiven old friends, family members, and even strangers, each one finding their own way to let go of past hurts. Maya saw that forgiveness was a deeply personal journey, unique to each person, but that it always led to a place of peace.

Finally, Eamon led Maya to a small stone bridge that spanned a narrow section of the river. The bridge was simple, yet it held an air of significance, as if it had seen countless travelers cross over, each one carrying their own stories and burdens.

Chapter 12: The Song of Belonging

Maya eagerly returned to *The Book of Endless Stories,* feeling its gentle magic tugging at her heart once more. She wondered what new adventure awaited her and which hidden corners of her own heart the book would help her discover. This time, as she turned the page, she saw an illustration of people gathered around a fire under a starlit sky, each one holding a musical instrument or singing. They were smiling, their faces glowing with joy and a sense of kinship. Before Maya could take another breath, she felt herself drifting, and when she opened her eyes, she found herself in a large, open clearing surrounded by trees.

The sky above was a deep midnight blue, filled with stars that seemed to twinkle brighter than she had ever seen before. A soft, warm breeze rustled the leaves, and the air was alive with the gentle hum of voices and laughter. Maya looked around, taking in the sight of people from all walks of life gathered together, each one carrying an instrument or a handmade object. They looked so different from one another, yet there was a quiet unity among them that felt like a comforting embrace.

"Welcome, Maya," a gentle voice said, drawing her attention. She turned and saw a woman with long, flowing hair and a serene expression. Her eyes sparkled like the stars above, and she wore a woven shawl decorated with symbols that seemed to shimmer in the firelight.

"My name is Liora," the woman said with a warm smile. "Tonight, we are here to celebrate the Song of Belonging, a song that connects us all. Each voice, each sound, is part of a greater melody, one that reminds us that we all belong."

Maya felt a surge of warmth in her chest. She had heard of songs that brought people together, but there was something different here—something deeper. It was as if the song itself was alive, weaving a thread of connection among everyone gathered in the clearing.

"What does it mean to belong?" Maya asked, her voice filled with wonder.

Liora's smile widened. "Belonging means being seen, being valued for who you are, and knowing that there is a place for you in the world. When we sing the Song of Belonging, we are reminded that we each have something unique to share, something only we can bring to the melody of life."

Maya felt her heart swell as she looked around at the people who were beginning to gather in a circle. Each one looked at ease, comfortable and happy, as if they had found a place where they truly belonged. She wondered what it would feel like to be part of something like this, to add her own voice to a song that connected everyone.

Liora led her to a space in the circle, and as Maya took her place, she felt a sense of anticipation building within her. She noticed that each person held something in their hands—a drum, a flute, a small bell, or even just their hands folded together. Each one was unique, and yet each one was essential to the gathering.

Liora raised her hands, and the clearing grew quiet. The stillness was filled with a quiet power, as if the air itself was waiting for the first note to be sung. Slowly, Liora began to hum a gentle melody, her voice low and rich, resonating through the clearing. One by one, others joined in, each adding their own voice, their own instrument, their own rhythm. The sounds blended together, forming a song that was both complex and beautiful, like a tapestry woven from countless individual threads.

Maya listened, enchanted. She felt each note reach into her heart, as if the song was speaking directly to her, inviting her to be part of it. She took a deep breath and, with a sense of both excitement and vulnerability, began to hum along softly. Her voice was quiet at first, blending with the others, but as she grew more confident, she let it grow stronger, letting her own unique tone join the melody.

As she sang, she felt a warmth spreading through her, a sense of being connected not just to the people in the clearing, but to something much larger, something timeless and boundless. She realized that each person's voice, each instrument, each beat was essential to the song, creating a harmony that was only possible because everyone was part of it.

As the song continued, Maya looked around at the faces of the people singing beside her. She saw a young girl with a bright smile, a man with wise, knowing eyes, and an elderly woman whose face was lined with years of life and laughter. She noticed that each person, though different in age, background, and appearance, had something unique to offer, and together they formed a melody that was rich and full of life.

Maya began to understand that belonging wasn't about being the same as others; it was about celebrating differences, about recognizing that each person's unique qualities contributed to the beauty of the whole. She felt her heart swell with gratitude as she realized that she, too, had a place in this melody, that her voice, no matter how quiet, was important.

The song shifted, growing softer, and Liora raised her hands again, signaling a pause. In the silence, she spoke, her voice filled with warmth and wisdom. "Belonging is not about fitting in; it is about being true to who you are. Each one of you is here because you bring something special to this circle, something that no one else can offer. This song, this melody, exists only because each of you has chosen to share yourselves with one another."

Liora invited everyone to share a story or a thought, something that came to mind as they sang together. One by one, people spoke, their voices soft yet filled with emotion. Some shared memories of times when they had felt alone, of times when they had longed to belong, while others spoke of moments when they had felt the warmth of connection, the joy of being part of something greater than themselves.

Maya listened, feeling each story settle into her heart like a note in the song. She realized that everyone, at some point, had felt the need to belong, the longing to be part of a community, to be valued for who they were. It was a universal feeling, one that connected them all.

Chapter 13: The Hidden Garden of Wonder

The air was thick with the scent of blossoms and fresh earth, and the faint, melodious hum of unseen creatures drifted through the air. The garden was enclosed by tall trees that formed a protective circle around it, their branches weaving together to form a canopy that filtered the sunlight into soft, dappled patterns on the ground. As she stepped further in, Maya noticed that every inch of the garden was teeming with life—flowers of every shade bloomed in clusters, insects buzzed from petal to petal, and small creatures scurried through the grass. It was as if the garden itself was breathing, alive in a way that filled her with awe.

"Welcome, Maya," a warm, gentle voice called out from the shadows of a large flowering bush. She turned to see a woman with eyes as green as the leaves around her and hair that seemed to blend with the flowers. She wore a simple dress adorned with vines and petals, and her presence radiated a calm and earthy wisdom.

"My name is Amira," the woman said, her smile soft and welcoming. "I am the keeper of the Hidden Garden of Wonder. Here, every plant, every creature, has its own unique beauty and purpose. This garden is a celebration of diversity, a place where all forms of life come together in harmony."

Maya's heart swelled as she looked around at the countless varieties of plants and animals, each one unique, each one contributing to the garden's vibrant tapestry. She could feel that this was no ordinary garden—it was a place where every part, no matter how small, played a vital role in creating the whole.

"What makes this garden so special?" Maya asked, her voice filled with wonder.

Amira knelt down beside a small, delicate flower with petals that shimmered like gemstones. "This garden is a symbol of unity in diversity," she explained. "Every flower, every creature, has a different shape, color, or sound, yet each one belongs here. Together, they create a beauty that could not exist if even one part were missing. Each life, each form, adds its own magic to the garden."

Maya felt a spark of understanding. She had seen gardens before, but none like this. In this hidden place, every leaf, every petal, every creature was valued, respected, and celebrated for its uniqueness. As she looked closer, she noticed that no two flowers were alike. Some were large and vibrant, others were small and soft, yet each one had its own kind of beauty, a beauty that contributed to the garden's harmony.

Amira gestured to a path winding through the garden, inviting Maya to explore. As she walked, she marveled at the countless varieties of plants and creatures around her. There were trees with leaves shaped like teardrops, bushes covered in golden blooms, and even a small cluster of glowing mushrooms that seemed to emit their own light. Each plant, each life, held its own special quality, and Maya could feel the harmony that existed between them.

As she continued, she noticed a cluster of bright orange flowers growing near a small pond. Their petals were wide and full, and they stood tall and proud, their faces turned toward the sun. Nearby, delicate white flowers with thin, star-shaped petals grew low to the ground, almost hidden in the grass. They were quiet, subtle, and seemed content to remain unnoticed.

Maya knelt down beside the white flowers, feeling a soft admiration for their gentle beauty. She turned to Amira, who had followed her. "These flowers are so small and quiet," she said thoughtfully. "But they're just as beautiful as the others."

Amira nodded, her eyes filled with understanding. "Every part of this garden has a role, Maya, just as every person has something unique to offer. Some flowers stand tall and catch the light, while others are subtle and hidden. Yet both are equally important. Each adds its own kind of beauty, its own essence to the garden."

Maya realized that this garden was a reminder of the value of diversity. It showed her that beauty could be found in both the bold and the quiet, in the bright and the soft. She felt a deep appreciation for the garden's harmony, a harmony that existed because every part was accepted and valued for what it was.

As they continued their walk, Maya noticed a small, shimmering pool nestled between two rocks. She peered into the water and saw tiny fish darting back and forth, their scales reflecting all the colors of the rainbow. They moved in graceful patterns, weaving around each other with a fluidity that looked like a dance. She could see that each fish had a different color and shape, yet they moved together as if guided by an invisible rhythm.

Amira smiled as she watched Maya's fascination. "These fish live together, each one different from the other, yet they move in harmony. They have learned to respect each other's movements, to dance together without colliding. It's a reminder that even in our differences, we can find ways to move together, to create something beautiful."

Maya felt a sense of wonder as she watched the fish, understanding that their dance was a reflection of the unity that existed throughout the garden. Each fish brought its own color, its own shape, but together they created a pattern that was mesmerizing and peaceful.

As they walked further, Maya noticed a tree with bark that was rough and textured, its branches twisted and knotted. It stood strong and tall, its roots digging deep into the earth. Nearby, a soft, moss-covered rock provided a place for small creatures to rest. Maya watched as a tiny bird flitted down to the rock, resting for a moment before flying off again. The tree, the rock, and the bird all seemed to fit together perfectly, each one contributing to the life of the garden.

Amira placed a gentle hand on the tree's trunk, her expression thoughtful. "This garden teaches us that strength and gentleness, boldness and quiet, all have their place. The tree and the rock each offer something unique, and together they create a home for many forms of life. Every part of this garden relies on the others, and without even one of them, the harmony would be incomplete."

Maya felt a deep respect for the garden, for the way each part supported the others, creating a balance that was both strong and delicate. She realized that the garden was like a community, each member contributing something valuable, each one essential to the whole.

As they walked back toward the center of the garden, Amira paused and gestured to a small cluster of flowers growing in a shaded corner. Their petals were pale, almost translucent, and they seemed to glow softly in the dim light. Maya felt drawn to them, sensing that they were special in some way.

"These flowers only bloom in the shade," Amira explained. "They are delicate and need protection from the sun, but their beauty is just as powerful as any other. They teach us that even those who may seem fragile have their own strength, their own place in the world."

Maya knelt down beside the flowers, feeling a sense of reverence for their quiet beauty. She realized that the garden was filled with life forms of every kind—strong and delicate, bold and gentle, each one valued, each one accepted.

As the day began to fade, Amira led Maya to a small clearing where a circle of stones surrounded a patch of soft grass. The stones were smooth and worn, and each one bore a different symbol, carved carefully into the surface. Amira gestured for Maya to sit, and as she settled down, she felt a sense of calm wash over her.

"This circle represents the unity of all life," Amira said, her voice soft and filled with wisdom. "Each symbol represents a different form of life in the garden, each one a unique part of the whole. This garden reminds us that diversity is not something to be merely tolerated; it is something to be cherished, something that brings strength and beauty to the world."

Maya closed her eyes, letting Amira's words settle into her heart. She understood now that the garden was more than just a collection of plants and animals. It was a symbol of the beauty of diversity, a reminder that every life had a purpose, a place in the world. She felt a deep gratitude for the lesson the garden had taught her, a lesson of unity, respect, and wonder.

Chapter 14: The Workshop of Dreams

The workshop was massive, with high, arched windows that let in streams of sunlight, illuminating the dust that floated gently in the air. Everywhere she looked, Maya saw people at work, each one focused intently on their own creation. Some were painting, others sculpting, and some were hunched over benches, carefully crafting intricate designs. There was an atmosphere of creativity that filled the room, a quiet energy that felt like a heartbeat, steady and alive.

"Welcome, Maya," a voice said, drawing her attention. She turned to see a tall, older man with silver hair and a kind, thoughtful face. He wore simple clothes covered in splashes of paint and wood shavings, evidence of years spent working with his hands. His eyes sparkled with warmth, and his presence radiated a calm assurance that made Maya feel instantly at ease.

"My name is Jonas," he said, smiling. "I am the Keeper of the Workshop of Dreams. Here, people come to shape their ideas, to bring their dreams to life through the work of their hands and the creativity of their minds."

Maya felt a thrill of excitement. She had always loved the idea of creating something, of transforming an idea into reality. She looked around the workshop, her gaze lingering on the various materials spread across tables and shelves—blocks of wood, pots of paint, bundles of fabric, and trays filled with metal and stone. Each material seemed to carry its own story, its own potential waiting to be uncovered.

Jonas gestured toward a bench nearby, inviting her to sit. "Every person who comes here brings a dream with them," he explained. "Some dreams are simple, others are complex. Some are personal, while others are meant to be shared with the world. But each one is unique, and each one requires care, patience, and vision to bring it to life."

Maya sat down, watching as he carefully picked up a small piece of wood and began to carve it with a knife, shaping it with practiced precision. "Creating something takes time," he said, his eyes focused on his work. "It requires dedication, but also an openness to discovery. Sometimes, the end result is different from what we imagined, and that's part of the magic."

As Maya watched him work, she noticed the sense of calm and purpose in his movements. She could see that he wasn't rushing, that each cut, each stroke of the knife was deliberate, as if he was allowing the piece to reveal itself gradually. She felt inspired, sensing that this workshop was not only a place for making things but also a place for nurturing dreams.

Jonas looked up and met her gaze. "Would you like to create something of your own?" he asked, his smile encouraging.

Maya nodded, feeling a mixture of excitement and uncertainty. She had never carved, painted, or sculpted before, and she wasn't sure where to begin. But Jonas's words gave her courage, and she reached for a small block of wood, feeling its rough surface beneath her fingers.

Jonas handed her a carving tool and showed her how to hold it, guiding her as she made her first tentative cuts. "There's no rush," he said gently. "Take your time, listen to the material, and let your hands guide you. Creativity is a conversation between you and your dream."

Maya began to carve, her movements slow and careful. At first, her cuts were uncertain, but as she continued, she felt a rhythm develop, a quiet connection between herself and the wood. Each cut revealed a new shape, a new possibility, and she found herself absorbed in the process, her worries and doubts fading into the background. She began to understand that creativity wasn't about perfection; it was about exploration, about giving herself permission to make mistakes and to learn from them.

As she worked, she noticed the people around her, each one absorbed in their own project. She saw a young girl painting a canvas with bold, sweeping strokes, her expression focused and intense. Nearby, an older woman was weaving a tapestry, her fingers moving with graceful precision as she wove colorful threads into intricate patterns. Each person was creating something different, yet there was a shared energy that filled the workshop, a sense of unity in their individual pursuits.

Maya realized that this was a place where dreams were honored, where people could bring their ideas to life without fear of judgment or failure. It was a place where each person's creativity was valued, where mistakes were part of the journey and where every creation, no matter how simple or complex, held a special beauty.

As she continued to carve, Maya thought about the dreams she held in her own heart. She had always wanted to make a difference, to share the lessons she had learned on her journeys through the book with others. She realized that this workshop was teaching her that dreams required patience and commitment, that they needed to be nurtured and shaped, just like the piece of wood she held in her hands.

Chapter 15: The Lake of Reflection

The air was crisp and cool, carrying the faint, earthy scent of the forest that bordered the lake. The sun was just beginning to set, casting a warm, golden glow across the water. Maya stood at the water's edge, looking out over the lake, mesmerized by its stillness. The water was so calm that it reflected the sky above with perfect clarity, creating an illusion of two worlds—one above and one below, joined together in a serene embrace.

"Welcome, Maya," a soft voice called out. She turned to see an elderly woman standing nearby. Her hair was silver, cascading down her shoulders, and her face was gentle and wise, marked with the quiet strength that comes from a life well-lived. She wore simple clothes, and in her hand, she held a small, smooth stone that she turned over thoughtfully.

"My name is Esme," the woman said with a smile, her voice as calm and steady as the lake itself. "I am the Keeper of the Lake of Reflection. Here, people come to see themselves more clearly, to look into the mirror of their own hearts."

Maya felt a surge of curiosity as she gazed at the lake, its surface so clear that it reflected her own image back to her with startling precision. She noticed the expression on her own face, the small details she rarely saw so clearly. It was as if the lake was inviting her to look deeper, to see herself not just as she appeared on the outside, but as she was on the inside.

"What do you mean by seeing ourselves clearly?" Maya asked, her voice filled with wonder.

Esme smiled knowingly and knelt down by the water's edge, motioning for Maya to join her. "This lake is a place of reflection, Maya, a place where people come to understand themselves better. Here, they can look into their hearts, see their own strengths and weaknesses, their hopes and fears. It is a place of honesty and acceptance."

Maya knelt beside her, feeling a sense of anticipation mixed with a hint of apprehension. She had learned many things on her journeys, but the idea of looking inward, of reflecting on herself, felt different, deeper somehow.

Esme held out the stone in her hand, offering it to Maya. "This stone is like a thought, a question, or a feeling," she explained. "When we toss it into the lake, it creates ripples, just as our thoughts and actions create ripples in our own lives. Watching the ripples helps us understand how each thought, each choice, affects the whole."

Maya took the stone, feeling its smooth surface cool against her skin. She gazed at the lake, then gently tossed the stone into the water. It landed with a soft splash, and she watched as ripples spread out across the lake, each one expanding in a perfect circle, reaching farther and farther until they faded into stillness once more.

As the ripples settled, Maya felt a calmness within herself, as if the lake's tranquility was seeping into her. She thought about the ripples, how each one affected the next, how they spread out across the surface, touching every part of the lake. She realized that her own thoughts, words, and actions were like those ripples, affecting not only herself but also the world around her.

"Reflection helps us see the impact of our actions," Esme said softly, her gaze focused on the lake. "Just as each ripple shapes the surface of the water, each choice we make shapes our own lives and the lives of those around us."

Maya felt a quiet understanding settle within her. She thought about the times when she had acted without thinking, the moments when her words or actions had created ripples that affected others, sometimes in ways she hadn't intended. She realized that reflection wasn't just about looking inward; it was about understanding how she connected with the world.

Esme placed a hand on her shoulder, her eyes warm and compassionate. "Would you like to walk with me, Maya?" she asked gently. "The lake has many secrets to share, if you're willing to listen."

Maya nodded, feeling a sense of openness and trust. Together, they began to walk along the edge of the lake, their footsteps soft on the earth. Esme spoke in a calm, measured tone, sharing stories of others who had come to the lake seeking clarity and understanding.

She spoke of a young man who had been burdened by regret, unable to forgive himself for mistakes he had made. He had come to the lake, hoping to find peace, to let go of the guilt that weighed on his heart. As he watched the ripples spread across the water, he began to understand that his mistakes were part of his journey, that they were lessons meant to guide him, not define him. Through reflection, he found the strength to forgive himself, to see his mistakes as stepping stones to growth.

Maya listened, feeling the depth of the young man's story resonate within her. She realized that forgiveness, both of oneself and others, was an essential part of reflection. It was a way of letting go, of freeing oneself from the burdens of the past.

As they continued their walk, they came across a woman sitting by the water's edge, her expression contemplative. Esme introduced her as Lina, and as they sat together, Lina shared her story. She had always felt uncertain about herself, unsure of her own worth and abilities. She had come to the lake seeking clarity, hoping to understand herself better.

"I looked into the water," Lina said softly, her gaze distant, "and I saw myself not as I thought others saw me, but as I truly am. I saw my strengths, my kindness, my resilience. I realized that I am enough, just as I am. This lake showed me that my worth isn't determined by others but by the truth I hold within myself."

Maya felt a warmth spread through her as she listened to Lina's words. She understood now that reflection was also about self-acceptance, about seeing oneself clearly and embracing both strengths and flaws. It was about finding value in who she was, rather than seeking validation from others.

Esme led Maya further along the lake, and they paused to watch a family nearby, each one looking into the water with thoughtful expressions. Esme explained that the family had come to the lake to strengthen their bond, to understand each other's hopes and fears. Through reflection, they found a deeper sense of unity, a connection that came from seeing one another's hearts.

Maya realized that reflection wasn't only a solitary journey; it was something that could bring people closer, helping them to see one another with empathy and understanding. She thought about her own family, about the times when she had struggled to see things from their perspectives, and she felt a new appreciation for the importance of connection.

"This circle is a place of acceptance, a place where people come to reflect on their journey, to find peace with their past and strength for the future," Esme said, her voice filled with quiet wisdom. "Reflection helps us see the whole picture, to understand where we've been and where we're going."

Maya closed her eyes, letting Esme's words sink in. She thought about her journey, about the lessons she had learned, the challenges she had faced. She realized that each experience, each moment of growth, was part of a larger picture, a journey of becoming who she was meant to be. She felt a deep sense of gratitude for the path she was on, for the people she had met, and for the wisdom she had gained.

Chapter 16: The Market of Generosity

The air was filled with the scent of fresh-baked bread, ripe fruits, and spices that made her mouth water. Maya looked around, her eyes wide with wonder as she took in the colorful scene before her. Stalls lined the cobblestone paths, each one bursting with goods—baskets of fresh produce, handwoven textiles, jars of honey, handmade trinkets, and more. People moved through the market with smiles on their faces, stopping to chat with vendors and share laughter with friends. There was a joyful, welcoming energy that filled the space, making Maya feel immediately at home.

"Welcome, Maya," a warm voice greeted her. She turned to see a middle-aged woman with a friendly smile and bright, curious eyes. Her clothes were simple but neat, and she carried a basket filled with various goods. She held herself with a gentle strength, and her presence radiated kindness and warmth.

"My name is Isla," the woman said, extending her hand in greeting. "I am one of the vendors here, and I also help welcome visitors to the Market of Generosity."

Maya shook her hand, feeling instantly connected to her. "Thank you," Maya said, her excitement bubbling over. "This market is so beautiful. It feels so alive!"

Isla chuckled, her eyes crinkling at the corners. "Yes, it truly is. This market is a place where people come not just to trade or buy, but to share, to give from the heart. Every item you see here has a story, a piece of the person who made it. This place thrives on generosity—each stall, each person is here to give something, to offer something meaningful."

Maya's curiosity grew as she looked around, realizing that this market was unlike any she had seen before. It was a place where people came to give as much as to receive, a place where generosity was woven into every interaction, every exchange. She felt a warmth growing in her chest as she watched the people around her, their smiles genuine and their words kind.

Isla gestured to a nearby stall filled with handmade scarves in every color imaginable. "Would you like to meet some of the people here?" she asked. "They each have something special to share."

Maya nodded eagerly, following Isla to the stall, where a man stood with a wide grin, his hands deftly folding one of his vibrant scarves. His clothes were simple, but he wore a scarf around his neck that was woven in intricate patterns of green and blue, matching the twinkle in his eye.

"This is Leo," Isla introduced him with a smile. "He's known for his scarves. People come from far and wide to get one of his creations."

Leo laughed, waving a hand dismissively. "Oh, don't listen to her, Maya," he said with a playful grin. "They're just simple scarves, nothing fancy."

Maya picked up one of the scarves, marveling at the softness of the fabric and the beauty of the design. "They're beautiful," she said, her voice filled with admiration. "You must put a lot of care into making them."

Leo's expression softened, his gaze thoughtful. "I do," he said. "Each scarf takes time, patience, and a little bit of heart. I believe that when you make something with love, it carries that love with it, and whoever wears it feels it too."

Maya felt a sense of awe as she listened to him. She understood now that generosity wasn't only about giving things; it was about giving a part of oneself, sharing one's own passion, care, and warmth with others. She realized that the scarf she held wasn't just a piece of fabric; it was a piece of Leo's heart, his gift to the world.

They moved on to another stall where a young woman with a warm smile was arranging jars of honey and small pots of jam. Her name was Nira, and she explained that she gathered honey from her family's beehives and made the jam from fruits grown in her own garden. Each jar sparkled in the sunlight, golden and inviting.

"People love your honey, Nira," Isla said with a wink. "They say it's the best in the market."

Nira laughed softly, her cheeks tinged with a blush. "I just like to share what I have," she said, her voice gentle. "Bees are such wonderful creatures, and they work so hard to make each drop of honey. I feel like it's a gift from them, and I just help pass it along."

Maya tasted a spoonful of honey that Nira offered her, its sweetness melting on her tongue. She felt the warmth of Nira's generosity, her desire to share something that was close to her heart, something she had nurtured with care. She realized that Nira's gift wasn't just the honey; it was the time, the effort, and the love she had put into gathering it and bringing it to the market. Through her honey, she was sharing a piece of herself.

As they continued through the market, Maya met a variety of people, each one offering something unique and personal. There was a woman who made beautiful pottery, each piece painted with delicate patterns inspired by the flowers in her garden. A young boy sold freshly baked bread that his grandmother had taught him to make, each loaf filled with warmth and comfort. An elderly man carved wooden figurines, each one capturing a different animal or scene from nature.

With each person Maya met, she felt her understanding of generosity deepen. She realized that generosity was more than just giving things away; it was about sharing something meaningful, something that came from the heart. Each gift was a reflection of the person who had created it, a part of themselves offered freely to others.

At one stall, Maya noticed a woman selling woven baskets, each one intricately designed and sturdy. The woman's name was Fara, and she greeted Maya with a warm smile, offering her a small basket as a gift. Maya accepted it gratefully, admiring the craftsmanship and beauty of the weave.

Fara explained that she had learned to make baskets from her mother, who had learned from her mother before her. "Each basket I make carries a piece of my family's history," she said softly. "It's my way of honoring them, of keeping their memory alive. When I give a basket to someone, I feel like I'm sharing a part of my family with them."

Maya felt a surge of emotion as she held the basket, realizing that it was more than just a container; it was a symbol of love, tradition, and memory. She understood that Fara's gift was not just a basket, but a piece of her heritage, a story woven into every strand. She saw that generosity could also be a way of sharing one's own history, a way of connecting others to the things that mattered most.

As the day continued, Maya saw countless acts of kindness and generosity. She watched as people shared laughter, exchanged stories, and offered gifts from the heart. She noticed that generosity didn't only come from the vendors; it was present in every interaction, in the small acts of kindness that filled the market. People helped each other carry heavy baskets, offered samples of their goods, and shared smiles and laughter freely.

Chapter 17: The Forest of Resilience

Maya opened *The Book of Endless Stories,* feeling the familiar sense of excitement and anticipation that each new page brought. Every journey had been a gift, each one filled with lessons and experiences that deepened her understanding of herself and the world around her. Today, as she turned the next page, she saw an illustration of a dense, ancient forest, filled with towering trees that reached up to the sky. The trees looked weathered and strong, their trunks thick and their branches stretching wide as if to protect everything below. She could feel the quiet strength of the forest through the image alone, and before she knew it, the world around her shifted, and she was standing at the edge of that very forest.

The air was cool and earthy, filled with the scent of moss, bark, and leaves. Rays of sunlight streamed down through the canopy, casting dappled shadows across the forest floor. The trees loomed above her, their branches weaving together like the arms of guardians watching over the land. There was a quiet power in the air, a strength that seemed to pulse from the ground itself, and Maya felt a sense of awe and reverence as she took in her surroundings.

"Welcome, Maya," a gentle yet firm voice called out, breaking the silence. She turned to see an older man approaching her, his face weathered like the bark of the trees, his eyes deep and wise. He wore simple clothes in earthy tones, blending almost seamlessly with the forest. His expression was calm, and he moved with the quiet confidence of someone who knew the forest well.

"My name is Rowan," he said, extending a hand in greeting. His voice was low and steady, filled with a quiet strength. "I am the Keeper of the Forest of Resilience. This forest is a place of endurance, of growth, and of learning to stand tall even in the face of challenges."

Maya shook his hand, feeling the roughness of his skin, a testament to years spent working with the earth. She looked around, her heart swelling with curiosity and respect. "What do you mean by resilience?" she asked, her voice filled with wonder.

Rowan gestured to the towering trees around them, his gaze thoughtful. "Resilience is the strength to endure, to continue growing despite the storms, despite the hardships. These trees have stood for centuries, weathering wind, rain, and drought. They bend but do not break. They adapt, they grow, and in doing so, they find their strength."

Maya looked up at the trees with a new appreciation, noticing the scars on their trunks, the way some branches twisted in unexpected directions. She could see that each tree had a story of its own, a story of survival and growth. She felt a deep admiration for their strength, their ability to endure whatever came their way.

Rowan led her deeper into the forest, and as they walked, he shared stories of resilience, tales of people who had come to the forest to find strength within themselves. He spoke of a young woman who had faced loss, her heart heavy with grief, and how she had come to the forest to find peace. She had walked among the trees, finding solace in their quiet strength, and over time, she had learned to carry her sorrow with grace, to let it become a part of her story without letting it define her.

Maya listened intently, feeling the power of Rowan's words. She realized that resilience was not about being unbreakable; it was about learning to bend without giving up, about finding a way to continue forward even when the path was difficult. She felt a quiet strength grow within her, inspired by the stories and the ancient wisdom of the forest.

As they walked, they came upon a tree that was bent and twisted, its trunk scarred and weathered. Rowan paused, placing a hand on the tree with a look of respect. "This tree has faced many storms," he said softly. "It has been struck by lightning, battered by wind, yet it still stands. It has found a way to survive, to grow in its own way."

Maya reached out, touching the rough bark, feeling the resilience of the tree beneath her fingers. She could see that it wasn't perfect, that it had scars and twists, but it stood tall nonetheless, a testament to its strength and determination. She realized that resilience wasn't about perfection; it was about perseverance, about finding beauty and strength in one's scars.

Rowan continued leading her through the forest, and they came upon a clearing where several young saplings were growing. The saplings were small, their trunks thin and delicate, yet they stood with a quiet determination, reaching for the sunlight. Rowan explained that these young trees were the next generation of the forest, each one learning to grow, to adapt to the conditions around them.

"Resilience is something we learn from those who came before us," Rowan said, his gaze resting on the saplings. "These young trees look to the older ones, finding guidance in their strength. They learn to bend with the wind, to dig their roots deep, to seek the light. It is a lesson passed down through the forest."

Maya felt a sense of connection as she looked at the saplings, understanding that resilience was something that grew within each of them, shaped by their experiences and the challenges they faced. She realized that resilience was not only about surviving; it was about growing, about reaching for the light even when the path was difficult.

They continued their journey, and as they walked, Rowan shared more stories. He spoke of a man who had faced failure and disappointment, who had come to the forest seeking a way to move forward. The man had walked among the trees, finding inspiration in their strength, and over time, he had learned to accept his failures, to see them as steps on his journey rather than as barriers.

As they walked further, they came upon a stream that flowed through the forest, its waters clear and cool. Rowan knelt by the stream, motioning for Maya to join him. He explained that the stream was a symbol of resilience, a reminder that water always found a way to move forward, even when blocked by stones or fallen branches.

"Water teaches us that resilience is about adaptability," Rowan said, his voice thoughtful. "It shows us that even when the path is blocked, we can find another way. Resilience is not rigid; it is fluid, flowing around obstacles, finding new paths."

Maya watched the stream, feeling a sense of calm and strength as she listened to the sound of the water. She understood now that resilience was not just about standing tall like the trees; it was also about being adaptable, about finding ways to move forward even when the path was unclear.

Chapter 18: The Tower of Understanding

As Maya sat down with *The Book of Endless Stories,* she felt a familiar thrill of excitement wash over her. Each journey in the book had left her with something new, something precious, and she wondered what today's adventure would teach her. She turned to the next page and saw an illustration of a tall, ancient tower reaching high into the clouds. The stone walls were worn and weathered, covered in vines and moss, yet it stood proud and strong, a testament to its age and resilience. At the top, windows looked out in every direction, offering a view of the landscape that seemed to stretch on forever. Maya felt herself drawn to the image, and within moments, the world around her shifted, and she found herself standing at the base of that very tower.

The tower loomed above her, its stone walls stretching toward the sky. The air was cool and filled with the faint scent of earth and moss, and she could hear the distant sound of birds calling to one another. She looked up at the tower's height, wondering what lay at the top, what mysteries and lessons it held within its ancient walls.

"Welcome, Maya," a voice called from nearby. She turned to see an elderly man approaching her, his face gentle and wise, marked by deep lines that spoke of years spent learning and observing. He wore simple clothes, a long tunic and a woolen scarf, and his eyes were kind and curious, as if he saw the world with a rare depth of understanding.

"My name is Elias," he said, inclining his head in greeting. "I am the Keeper of the Tower of Understanding. This tower has stood for centuries, watching over the land, a place where people come to gain a broader perspective, to see beyond their own experiences."

Maya felt a surge of curiosity as she looked up at the tower again. "What do you mean by seeing beyond our own experiences?" she asked, her voice filled with wonder.

Elias smiled, his gaze thoughtful. "Understanding is about looking at the world through many lenses, seeing not only with your eyes but with your heart and mind. Each level of this tower offers a different perspective, a new way of understanding the world and the people in it."

Maya nodded, feeling a spark of anticipation. She had always believed in the importance of empathy and compassion, but something about the tower intrigued her, as if it held secrets that could deepen her understanding of others. She felt ready to explore, to climb and discover what each level had to teach her.

Elias led her to a stone staircase winding up the inside of the tower, and together they began to climb. The first few steps were steep, the stones cool beneath her feet, and she could feel the air grow quieter, as if the tower itself was a place of deep thought and reflection.

As they reached the first level, Elias paused, gesturing to a large window that looked out over a village below. The view was clear, and Maya could see people moving about, going about their daily lives. There were children playing, merchants setting up their stalls, and elders sitting together in conversation. She could hear faint sounds of laughter and chatter, a soft hum of life below.

"From here, you can see the lives of others, a glimpse into their daily experiences," Elias explained. "Understanding begins with observation, with seeing others as they are, without judgment. It is about taking a step back from your own life and truly witnessing others, understanding that each person has their own story."

Maya felt a sense of wonder as she watched the people below. She thought about how each person had their own dreams, struggles, and moments of joy, each life filled with experiences she could only imagine. She realized that understanding others required her to look beyond her own perspective, to see the world through different eyes, even if only for a moment.

Elias nodded approvingly, sensing her realization. "Let's continue," he said, leading her back to the staircase. They climbed higher, the air growing cooler and the light softer as they moved up the winding steps.

At the next level, Elias guided her to another window, this one looking out over a vast forest stretching far into the horizon. The trees were tall and ancient, their branches woven together in a tapestry of green. Maya could see birds flying among the trees, their movements graceful and free.

"Nature has its own wisdom," Elias said softly, his voice filled with reverence. "Understanding extends beyond people; it includes the world around us, the environment, the ecosystems that support life. Each tree, each creature has a purpose, a role in the balance of life. Understanding means recognizing our connection to nature, our responsibility to protect and honor it."

Maya felt a deep respect as she looked out over the forest, realizing that understanding wasn't only about people; it was about appreciating the intricate web of life that sustained them all. She felt a surge of gratitude for the earth, for the beauty and strength of the natural world, and she understood that true understanding required a respect for all forms of life.

They climbed higher, reaching a level with a view of the mountains, their peaks covered in snow, stretching toward the sky. The landscape was rugged and majestic, filled with a sense of timelessness. Elias gestured for her to look out, his eyes filled with thought.

"Each person's life is like a mountain range," he said, his voice calm and reflective. "We each have our peaks and valleys, our highs and lows. Understanding others means recognizing that each person faces their own challenges, their own struggles. It is about honoring their journey, respecting the path they walk, even if it is different from our own."

As they climbed further, Elias paused at a level with a view of a vast ocean stretching into the distance, its surface sparkling under the sun. The waves moved gently, each one following the other in a rhythm that was both calming and powerful.

"The ocean teaches us about depth," Elias said, his gaze steady. "People are like the ocean; there is so much beneath the surface, hidden layers, thoughts, and emotions. Understanding others means acknowledging these depths, knowing that what we see is only a part of who they are. It is about being open to the unknown, to the parts of others that we may never fully understand."

Maya watched the waves, feeling the truth of his words. She realized that understanding required humility, an acceptance that there would always be things she didn't know, parts of people's hearts that were hidden from view. She felt a quiet respect for the mystery of others, for the depth of each person's soul.

Chapter 19: The Fountain of Kindness

Maya had walked through gardens, climbed towers, and crossed bridges, each journey teaching her something new and beautiful about the world and herself. She wondered what new insights awaited her this time. Turning to the next page, she found an illustration of a serene courtyard with a fountain at its center. The fountain was simple yet elegant, and from it flowed crystal-clear water that sparkled under the sunlight. Trees surrounded the fountain, their leaves casting dappled shadows across the stones, and nearby, flowers bloomed in vibrant colors, filling the air with a gentle fragrance. Before she knew it, she was standing in that very courtyard.

The air was warm and peaceful, filled with the soft murmur of water as it flowed from the fountain and the chirping of birds hidden in the branches above. The courtyard felt calm and inviting, as if it were a place meant for reflection, for moments of quiet and thoughtfulness. Maya walked toward the fountain, feeling a pull in her heart, a sense that this place held something special, something meant just for her.

"Welcome, Maya," a gentle voice said, breaking the silence. She turned to see a woman approaching her. The woman had a soft, radiant smile, and her eyes were filled with kindness and wisdom. She wore a flowing robe in hues of soft pink and lavender, and her movements were graceful and calm.

"My name is Althea," the woman said, her voice as warm as the sunlight that bathed the courtyard. "I am the Keeper of the Fountain of Kindness. Here, we celebrate the power of kindness, the gentle strength that brings light and warmth to the world."

Maya felt a spark of warmth in her heart as she looked at the fountain, its water clear and pure, flowing endlessly from the center. "What makes kindness so powerful?" she asked, her voice filled with curiosity.

Althea's smile softened, and she gestured to the fountain. "Kindness is like water, Maya. It flows freely, nourishing everything it touches. It may seem gentle, but it has the power to shape lives, to bring comfort, and to create connections. Kindness is the simplest gift, yet it can change the world."

Maya nodded, feeling the truth of Althea's words settle within her. She looked into the fountain, watching as the water sparkled in the sunlight, its gentle flow creating ripples that spread out across the surface. She realized that kindness, like the water, had a quiet strength, a power that went beyond words.

Althea led her to a stone bench near the fountain, inviting her to sit. As they sat together, Althea began to share stories of kindness, tales of people who had come to the fountain seeking healing, comfort, and connection. She spoke of a young boy who had been lost and afraid, who had found comfort in a stranger's smile and a helping hand. Through that simple act of kindness, the boy had felt seen, valued, and cared for, and it had given him the courage to keep going.

Maya listened, feeling a deep appreciation for the beauty of kindness. She thought about the times when a kind word, a small gesture, had lifted her own heart, making her feel less alone, more connected to the world around her. She realized that kindness didn't have to be grand or elaborate; even the smallest acts could carry immense power, offering warmth and light to those who needed it.

As they sat by the fountain, a young woman approached, her face filled with a mix of uncertainty and hope. She introduced herself as Lila and explained that she had come to the fountain because she felt isolated, disconnected from those around her. She shared that she often felt invisible, as if no one truly saw her, and that she longed for a sense of belonging.

Althea listened with a gentle, understanding smile. She reached out and placed a hand on Lila's shoulder, her touch soft and reassuring. "You are seen, Lila," she said softly. "Kindness begins with acknowledgment, with letting someone know that they matter, that they are valued just as they are."

Maya watched as Lila's face softened, a hint of relief and gratitude in her eyes. She saw how Althea's kindness, her willingness to listen and offer comfort, had already made a difference. She realized that kindness wasn't just about doing something for others; it was about being present, about truly seeing them and offering a moment of genuine connection.

Lila thanked Althea, her smile brighter, and she left with a sense of hope and warmth that had not been there before. Maya felt a deep sense of respect for Althea's kindness, for her ability to make someone feel seen and valued with just a few gentle words.

As they continued sitting by the fountain, Althea shared more stories, each one illustrating the power of kindness. She spoke of a man who had been carrying a heavy burden of guilt and regret, who had found healing in the kindness of a friend who forgave him without judgment. Through that kindness, the man had found the strength to forgive himself, to let go of his guilt and find peace.

Maya felt a warmth spreading through her as she listened, understanding that kindness had the power to heal, to mend broken hearts and lift heavy burdens. She realized that kindness could be a balm, a source of comfort and strength that helped people find their way forward, even when the path seemed dark and uncertain.

They were soon joined by a mother and her young daughter, who came to the fountain to offer flowers as a gesture of gratitude. The mother explained that her daughter had been ill, and during that difficult time, neighbors and friends had shown them countless acts of kindness—bringing food, offering to help with chores, and simply being there to listen and offer support. Those acts of kindness had made all the difference, reminding them that they were not alone, that they were part of a caring community.

Chapter 20: The Harbor of Peace

Boats of various shapes and sizes floated in the harbor, their sails lowered as they rested peacefully. In the distance, a lighthouse stood tall, its light a warm glow against the horizon. A feeling of calmness and serenity washed over her, and in the blink of an eye, she found herself standing at the edge of that very harbor.

The air was cool and fresh, carrying the faint scent of salt and seaweed. Gentle waves lapped against the shore, creating a rhythm that was both soothing and steady. The sky above was a deep blue, with streaks of pink and orange stretching across it as the sun began to dip toward the horizon. Maya took a deep breath, feeling the peaceful energy of the harbor settle within her, as though the place itself were a refuge from the noise and rush of the world.

"Welcome, Maya," a soft voice said from nearby. She turned to see a tall woman approaching her. The woman's face was calm and serene, her eyes gentle and kind, as if she carried a quiet strength within her. She wore a simple dress that flowed in the breeze, and a light scarf was wrapped around her shoulders.

"My name is Selene," the woman said with a smile. "I am the Keeper of the Harbor of Peace. This is a place where people come to find rest, to leave behind the burdens they carry and find stillness within."

Maya felt an immediate connection to Selene, drawn to the quiet strength and warmth she radiated. "What does it mean to find peace?" she asked, her voice soft with wonder.

Selene's smile grew, and she gestured to the harbor. "Peace is a quietness within, a state of balance and harmony. It doesn't mean there are no storms, but it is the calm that remains even when storms come. Peace is the strength to let go, to be still, to trust in the ebb and flow of life."

Maya nodded, feeling the truth of Selene's words resonate within her. She looked out over the water, watching as the gentle waves moved in rhythm, each one blending seamlessly into the next. She realized that peace, like the harbor, wasn't about escaping from challenges or difficulties; it was about finding a place of stillness and acceptance within herself.

Selene led Maya to a stone bench overlooking the harbor, inviting her to sit. As they sat together, Selene shared stories of peace, of people who had come to the harbor seeking refuge, hoping to find a sense of calm amid the storms of their lives. She spoke of a fisherman who had once come to the harbor, his heart weighed down by worry for his family, by fears of the future. Through the harbor's stillness, he had learned to release his worries, to find trust in life's natural rhythms and the strength within himself.

Maya listened, feeling a deep respect for the fisherman's journey. She thought about the times when she had felt weighed down by her own worries, moments when her mind had been filled with questions and uncertainties. She realized that peace wasn't about avoiding those feelings but about accepting them, letting them flow through her without allowing them to take over her heart.

As they sat by the harbor, a young woman approached, her face filled with a mixture of sadness and relief. She introduced herself as Rina and explained that she had come to the harbor to find peace after a difficult loss. She shared how she had been holding onto her grief, unable to move forward, feeling as if her sadness had become a weight she could not carry.

Selene listened with a compassionate expression, nodding gently as Rina spoke. "Peace is not the absence of pain," Selene said softly. "It is the ability to hold space for your pain, to let it be part of your story without letting it define you. It is the strength to let go, not of love, but of sorrow, to find a place within yourself where both peace and memory can exist together."

Maya watched as Rina's face softened, a quiet understanding settling over her. She saw how Selene's words had offered comfort, had helped Rina see that peace didn't mean forgetting or erasing her feelings but allowing them to be, without holding them too tightly. Maya realized that peace was a kind of strength, a way of holding onto memories and letting go of pain.

Rina thanked Selene, her face brighter, and she left with a sense of calm that had not been there before. Maya felt a deep appreciation for the quiet wisdom that Selene carried, for her ability to guide others toward peace through gentle words and understanding.

As the day continued, Selene shared more stories, each one a testament to the power of peace. She spoke of a sailor who had come to the harbor, his heart filled with restlessness and frustration, feeling as if he could never find his place in the world. He had walked along the harbor's edge, watching the boats float gently on the water, each one at rest, each one finding stillness in the harbor. Through the harbor's calm, he had found a sense of belonging, a quiet understanding that peace was not a place he needed to find but a feeling he could cultivate within himself.

They were soon joined by a family who came to the harbor to spend time together. The parents sat with their two children, watching the boats and listening to the waves. Selene explained that the family had come to the harbor to find a sense of unity, to reconnect after a time of challenges and misunderstandings. Through the harbor's peace, they had found a new sense of harmony, a reminder that peace could be found not only in stillness but in the presence of those they loved.

Chapter 21: The Garden of Curiosity

The scent of fresh soil and blooming flowers filled the air, mingling with the warmth of the sun that bathed the garden in golden light. Everything around her felt alive and inviting, as if the plants themselves were calling her to explore, to discover their secrets. Maya felt a surge of excitement as she looked around, her heart racing with curiosity, wondering what mysteries lay hidden in the heart of the garden.

"Welcome, Maya," a cheerful voice called from nearby. She turned to see a young woman with a friendly smile approaching her. The woman wore a colorful dress, its fabric covered in floral patterns that matched the vibrant colors of the garden. Her hair was tied back with a scarf, and her eyes sparkled with a playful, adventurous light.

"My name is Zara," the woman said, extending her hand. "I am the Keeper of the Garden of Curiosity. This garden is a place where questions grow, where wonders unfold, and where there is always something new to learn."

Maya felt an instant connection to Zara, sensing her lively spirit and boundless enthusiasm. "What does it mean to be curious?" Maya asked, her voice brimming with wonder.

Zara's smile widened as she gestured to the garden. "Curiosity is a hunger for understanding, a desire to know more. It's what drives us to ask questions, to explore, to see the world with fresh eyes. Curiosity is like the sun—it gives life to everything it touches, allowing us to grow and discover new things about ourselves and the world."

Maya nodded, feeling the truth of Zara's words echo within her. She looked at the garden, noticing the countless plants, each one unique, each one different from the others. She realized that curiosity was a force that led people to explore the unknown, to venture beyond what they already knew, and to embrace the mysteries that lay waiting to be uncovered.

Zara led her along a winding path that curved through the garden, stopping at a patch of tall, vibrant flowers with deep red petals that seemed to shimmer in the sunlight. She knelt beside one of the flowers, carefully examining its petals and the intricate patterns within them.

"Each flower, each plant in this garden has a story," Zara explained, her voice filled with admiration. "Curiosity teaches us to look closely, to pay attention to the details. It encourages us to ask questions and see beauty in the smallest things. When we are curious, we see the world in ways we never imagined."

Maya leaned in, studying the flower closely. She noticed tiny veins running through each petal, lines of color that she had never noticed in a flower before. She felt a sense of awe as she realized that even the smallest details held wonders, that each flower was a world unto itself, filled with secrets that could only be uncovered through patience and curiosity.

They continued their walk through the garden, and Zara shared stories of people who had come to the garden seeking knowledge, understanding, or inspiration. She spoke of a scientist who had spent hours observing a simple plant, finding inspiration in its resilience, in the way it adapted to survive and thrive. Through his curiosity, he had discovered new ways to help plants grow, ways that would benefit countless people around the world.

Maya felt a surge of admiration for the scientist, understanding that curiosity was not just a fleeting interest but a deep commitment to learning, to seeing things as they were and as they could be. She realized that curiosity was a path to discovery, one that led people to push boundaries, to expand their knowledge and understanding.

As they walked, they came upon a small pond, its surface calm and clear, reflecting the sky above. Fish swam lazily just below the surface, their scales catching the sunlight in flashes of color. Zara knelt by the pond, her gaze thoughtful.

"Curiosity is also about asking why," she said softly. "It's about wondering what lies beneath the surface, what causes things to be the way they are. When we ask why, we open doors to new possibilities, to answers that we might not have considered before."

Maya looked into the pond, feeling a sense of wonder as she watched the fish move gracefully through the water. She thought about the questions that curiosity inspired, questions that led people to look deeper, to seek knowledge and understanding not just on the surface, but in the layers beneath. She realized that curiosity was a bridge to understanding, a way of peeling back the layers of the world to reveal its mysteries.

Zara continued guiding her through the garden, showing her plants with unique textures, leaves that curled and twisted, fruits of unusual shapes and colors. Each one was a marvel, each one a mystery that invited her to wonder, to ask questions and seek answers.

As they walked, a young boy joined them, his face filled with excitement. He introduced himself as Theo and explained that he had come to the garden because he loved learning about insects and animals. He shared that he often came to observe the different creatures that lived among the plants, each one a tiny world of its own.

Zara smiled, her eyes filled with pride. "Curiosity opens our eyes to the richness of life," she said warmly. "When we are curious, we see each creature, each life form, as unique and important. Curiosity reminds us that there is always more to learn, more to appreciate."

Maya watched as Theo pointed out a small caterpillar crawling along a leaf, his excitement infectious. She realized that curiosity encouraged people to look closely, to see the wonder in things they might otherwise overlook. She felt a newfound appreciation for the beauty and complexity of life, for the countless details that curiosity allowed her to see and understand.

As the day continued, Zara led her to a small alcove filled with books and maps. Shelves were lined with journals and sketches, each one a record of someone's observations and discoveries in the garden. Zara explained that these books were filled with questions, with thoughts and ideas that people had recorded in their pursuit of knowledge.

"Curiosity is a journey," Zara said, her voice filled with reverence. "Each question we ask leads to another, each answer opening doors to new mysteries. Curiosity keeps us moving forward, reminding us that there is always more to discover, more to understand."

Maya felt a sense of wonder as she looked at the shelves, realizing that curiosity was a never-ending journey, one that took people to new places, new ideas, and new understandings. She understood that curiosity was like a river, constantly flowing, always leading to something new.

As the sun began to set, casting a warm, golden light over the garden, Maya felt a deep sense of gratitude for the lessons she had learned. She understood now that curiosity was more than just a desire to know; it was a way of seeing the world, a way of embracing the unknown with wonder and excitement.

Zara placed a gentle hand on her shoulder, her eyes filled with kindness and understanding. "Remember, Maya," she said softly, "curiosity is a gift, a light that guides us to new places, new ideas, and new truths. It is a path that leads us to understanding, to growth, and to a life filled with wonder."

Chapter 22: The Cave of Dreams

The air was cool and filled with a faint scent of earth and stone, with a slight breeze that carried whispers, as if voices from long ago were echoing from within. She took a step forward, her heart racing with excitement and a hint of trepidation. She felt as if she was about to uncover something ancient, something that had been waiting for her for a long time. The cave was dimly lit by an ethereal glow that seemed to come from nowhere and everywhere at once, illuminating the walls and casting soft shadows that danced and shifted as she moved forward.

"Welcome, Maya," a soft voice said, breaking the silence. She turned to see a figure emerge from the shadows. It was an older woman, her face lined with age and wisdom, her eyes twinkling with warmth and understanding. She wore a robe of deep blue that flowed around her like water, and her presence radiated a calm, steady strength that put Maya at ease.

"My name is Lyra," the woman said with a gentle smile. "I am the Keeper of the Cave of Dreams. This is a place where dreams take form, where hopes and desires are given space to grow and take root. It is a place of reflection, imagination, and transformation."

Maya felt a surge of excitement as she looked around the cave, noticing that the walls were covered with symbols and markings, each one unique, each one hinting at a story or a mystery. She could feel the energy of the cave around her, as if it held a thousand untold stories, a thousand dreams waiting to be discovered.

"What does it mean to dream?" Maya asked, her voice filled with wonder.

Lyra's eyes softened, and she gestured to the cave around them. "Dreaming is the act of envisioning something beyond what is, of reaching into the depths of your heart and mind to imagine new possibilities. Dreams are the seeds of hope, the whispers of our innermost desires. They guide us, inspire us, and remind us of what is possible."

Maya nodded, feeling the truth of Lyra's words settle within her. She looked around the cave, sensing that each shadow, each symbol, was a dream that had once been held close by someone, a hope or a desire that had shaped their journey. She realized that dreaming was more than just wishing for something; it was an act of courage, a commitment to envision a future that had yet to be born.

Lyra led her deeper into the cave, and as they walked, she began to share stories of dreams, tales of people who had come to the cave seeking inspiration, clarity, or direction. She spoke of a young artist who had come to the cave feeling lost, uncertain of her path. Through the cave's quiet stillness, she had found the courage to listen to her own heart, to reconnect with her passion and create art that reflected her true self. Her dream had been to express herself honestly, and through the cave's guidance, she had found the strength to do so.

Maya listened, feeling a deep admiration for the artist's journey. She thought about her own dreams, the hopes and aspirations she held within her heart, and she realized that dreams weren't just about achieving something; they were about finding purpose, about connecting with the deepest parts of herself. She understood that dreaming required vulnerability, a willingness to listen to her own desires and to honor them.

As they continued deeper into the cave, they came upon a series of stones arranged in a circle on the ground. Each stone was smooth and polished, and on each one, a different symbol was carved. Lyra gestured for Maya to sit, and as she did, she felt a sense of calm settle over her, a feeling of being connected to something larger than herself.

"These stones are markers of dreams that have been pursued, journeys that have been taken," Lyra explained. "Each symbol represents a person's dream, a goal they held close to their heart. These dreams have shaped lives, given people strength, and guided them on their paths. Dreams are like stars; they light the way, even when the road is dark."

Maya felt a quiet reverence as she looked at the stones, each one a testament to someone's courage, someone's vision. She realized that dreams had the power to shape lives, to give people direction and meaning, even when the path was difficult. She understood that dreams weren't just about reaching a destination; they were about the journey, about the growth and transformation that came from pursuing something meaningful.

Lyra led her to another part of the cave where a large pool of water lay still and undisturbed, its surface like glass. The water reflected the soft glow of the cave, creating a serene and magical atmosphere. Lyra invited Maya to kneel by the water's edge, and as she did, she could see her own reflection, clear and calm.

"This pool is a mirror of dreams," Lyra said softly. "It shows us our innermost desires, the hopes we hold close, the visions that guide us. It is a place where we can see ourselves as we truly are, where we can embrace our dreams and find the courage to pursue them."

Maya gazed into the pool, feeling a sense of wonder as she saw her own face reflected back at her. She thought about her dreams, the hopes she carried in her heart, and she felt a quiet determination grow within her. She realized that her dreams were a part of her, a reflection of her true self, and that pursuing them was an act of self-love, a way of honoring who she was.

As she continued to look into the pool, images began to form on the water's surface, visions of people pursuing their dreams, each one filled with purpose and passion. She saw a musician playing a song that moved people to tears, an inventor creating something that helped others, a teacher inspiring her students to believe in themselves. Each image was a testament to the power of dreams, a reminder that following one's passions could bring light and joy to the world.

Lyra placed a gentle hand on her shoulder, her gaze warm and encouraging. "Dreams are gifts we give to ourselves and to the world," she said softly. "When we pursue our dreams, we bring our unique light into the world, creating something that no one else can. Dreams are expressions of our soul, reflections of our deepest truths."

Maya felt a surge of inspiration as she listened to Lyra's words. She realized that her dreams were not just for herself; they were a way of contributing to the world, of sharing her unique gifts and talents with others. She understood that pursuing her dreams was an act of bravery, a commitment to live authentically and fully.

They continued exploring the cave, and Lyra shared more stories of people who had followed their dreams, each one a tale of courage, resilience, and hope. She spoke of a young man who had dreamed of helping others, who had become a healer, bringing comfort and strength to those in need. She spoke of a woman who had dreamed of exploring the world, who had traveled to distant lands and returned with stories and wisdom to share.

As they reached the end of the cave, Lyra led her to a small altar where a single candle burned, its flame steady and bright. Lyra explained that the candle represented the light of dreams, a reminder that even the smallest spark could illuminate the darkness, guiding her forward.

Chapter 23: The River of Change

Maya turned to the next page, she saw an illustration of a wide, flowing river that stretched as far as her eyes could see. The river sparkled under the sunlight, its waters moving swiftly in some places and gently in others, winding its way through forests and valleys, past towering cliffs and quiet fields. There was something captivating about the river, an energy that seemed both calm and powerful, as if it held within it the secret of life itself. The scene filled her with a quiet awe, and before she knew it, she was standing on the bank of that very river.

The air was fresh and cool, carrying the earthy scent of wet leaves and moss, and the sound of the rushing water filled her ears, a steady rhythm that felt like the heartbeat of the land. She looked out over the river, its surface shimmering with the light of the sun, each ripple and wave catching the light in a unique way. Maya felt a sense of wonder as she watched the river flow, its endless movement a reminder of the passage of time, of the changes that life inevitably brings.

"Welcome, Maya," a voice said softly. She turned to see an older man standing nearby. He wore simple, comfortable clothes, and his face was gentle, marked by deep lines that spoke of wisdom and experience. His eyes were warm and kind, filled with the quiet strength of someone who had weathered many storms.

"My name is Rian," he said with a smile. "I am the Keeper of the River of Change. This river is a place of transformation, a reminder that life is constantly moving, evolving, and shifting. Change is a natural part of our journey, a force that shapes us and helps us grow."

Maya felt a connection to Rian immediately, drawn to his calm presence and his thoughtful demeanor. "What does it mean to embrace change?" she asked, her voice filled with curiosity.

Rian's gaze softened as he looked out over the river. "Embracing change means being open to the flow of life, to the twists and turns, the unknowns and uncertainties. It means letting go of what is no longer needed and welcoming what comes next. The river flows because it is always moving, always adapting. To embrace change is to find peace in movement, to trust that each change is a part of a greater journey."

Maya nodded, feeling the truth of Rian's words settle within her. She looked at the river, watching as it moved around rocks and trees, finding its way over and under obstacles, flowing with a grace and strength that seemed both gentle and unbreakable. She realized that change was like the river, a force that carried her forward, shaping her path and guiding her through the landscapes of her life.

Rian led her to a large rock by the river's edge, inviting her to sit with him. As they sat together, Rian shared stories of change, tales of people who had come to the river seeking guidance, strength, and understanding. He spoke of a young woman who had struggled with letting go of her past, who had felt bound by memories and regrets that kept her from moving forward. Through the river's gentle guidance, she had learned to release her burdens, to let her past flow away like leaves carried by the current, finding freedom in the openness of change.

Maya listened intently, feeling a deep respect for the young woman's journey. She thought about her own experiences, the times when she had clung to familiar things, to memories or routines, afraid of the unknowns that change could bring. She realized that embracing change required trust, a willingness to let go and allow life to unfold in new ways.

As they sat by the river, a young man approached, his face marked by a mixture of excitement and nervousness. He introduced himself as Leo and explained that he had come to the river because he was facing a major life decision. He shared how he was torn between staying in a place he loved and pursuing a new opportunity that both thrilled and scared him.

Rian listened with a gentle understanding, nodding as Leo spoke. "The river flows forward, always moving, always adapting," he said softly. "Change brings with it uncertainty, but it also brings growth, new experiences, and possibilities. To embrace change is to trust that each decision, each step, will lead you to where you are meant to be."

Maya watched as Leo's face softened, a look of clarity and acceptance settling over him. She saw how Rian's words had offered him a sense of peace, a reminder that change, though uncertain, was a part of life's natural rhythm. She realized that change wasn't something to fear; it was a journey of exploration, a chance to grow and discover new aspects of herself.

Leo thanked Rian, his face brighter, and he left with a newfound sense of purpose and courage. Maya felt a deep admiration for Rian's wisdom, for his ability to guide others toward acceptance and trust in the flow of life.

As the day continued, Rian shared more stories, each one a testament to the power of change. He spoke of an elder who had come to the river, his heart heavy with sorrow after losing someone dear to him. Through the river's calming presence, he had found solace, learning to let his grief flow like the water, to release his pain without losing his love and memories.

Maya felt a warmth spreading through her as she listened, understanding that change was a part of all things, a force that could bring healing and renewal. She realized that change didn't mean forgetting; it was a way of carrying memories and experiences forward, allowing them to become part of who she was.

They were soon joined by a family who came to the river to share a picnic by its banks. The parents explained that they often brought their children here to teach them about the cycles of nature, about how life changes and grows just as the river flows and moves. Maya watched as the family sat together, their faces relaxed and content as they listened to the gentle sound of the water.

Rian smiled as he watched the family. "The river teaches us about continuity, about how each moment flows into the next, creating a journey that is both familiar and new. Change is a part of life, a rhythm that guides us and helps us grow."

As the afternoon turned to evening, Rian led Maya to a quiet pool where the water was calm and still, reflecting the colors of the sunset. He explained that this pool was a place of reflection, a reminder that change often began with looking within, with understanding her own desires and fears.

Maya knelt by the pool, gazing into its clear depths. She thought about the changes she had experienced in her life, the moments of uncertainty and growth, the times when she had stepped into the unknown. She realized that each change had brought her closer to herself, had helped her understand her own heart and mind.

Chapter 24: The Path of Compassion

Along the path, Maya noticed symbols and shapes, gentle reminders that seemed to whisper messages of kindness, patience, and understanding. The path felt inviting, as if it had been waiting for her, encouraging her to walk its length and discover its mysteries. With a gentle tug, she felt herself transported, and in the next instant, she stood at the beginning of that very path.

The air was filled with a gentle breeze, carrying the scent of blossoms and fresh earth, and the sound of birdsong filled the space around her. The path stretched before her, winding through groves of trees and clusters of flowers that seemed to dance in the sunlight. Each step she took felt light and easy, as if the path itself was guiding her forward, encouraging her to explore and discover what lay ahead.

"Welcome, Maya," a voice said softly from nearby. She turned to see a woman with a serene, kind expression approaching her. The woman's face was gentle, her eyes filled with warmth and compassion. She wore a simple robe in soft, earthy tones, and her presence radiated a calm, comforting energy.

"My name is Sari," the woman said with a gentle smile. "I am the Keeper of the Path of Compassion. This path is a place where people come to understand the power of kindness, empathy, and love. Compassion is a gift we give to others and ourselves, a way of connecting and understanding that brings healing and unity."

Maya felt a deep respect for Sari, sensing the quiet strength and kindness that radiated from her. "What does it mean to walk the path of compassion?" she asked, her voice filled with wonder.

Sari's smile grew as she gestured to the path before them. "To walk the path of compassion is to open your heart to the suffering and joys of others, to offer kindness and understanding without judgment. Compassion is a bridge that connects us, a way of seeing ourselves in others. It is a journey of empathy, a commitment to bring warmth and light wherever we go."

Maya nodded, feeling the truth of Sari's words settle within her. She looked at the path, noticing the small stones and flowers that bordered its edges, each one unique and beautiful in its own way. She realized that compassion was like the path itself, a way of moving forward with love and understanding, of seeing beauty and value in every person she met.

Sari began to walk along the path, and Maya followed, her heart open and her mind calm. As they walked, Sari shared stories of compassion, tales of people who had come to the path seeking understanding, healing, and connection. She spoke of a young mother who had come to the path feeling overwhelmed and lost, struggling to find balance and strength. Through the path's gentle guidance, she had found compassion for herself, learning to be patient and kind to her own heart as she navigated the challenges of life.

Maya listened, feeling a deep admiration for the young mother's journey. She thought about her own experiences, the times when she had been hard on herself, when she had felt weighed down by expectations and self-criticism. She realized that compassion wasn't just something she offered to others; it was a kindness she needed to show herself as well.

As they continued walking, they came upon a bench overlooking a field of wildflowers, their colors bright and cheerful under the sunlight. Sari gestured for Maya to sit, and as they settled, she noticed an elderly man sitting nearby, his face marked by years of experience, his eyes kind and wise. He introduced himself as Johan and shared that he had come to the path to find peace and forgiveness.

Johan explained that he had held onto anger and resentment for many years, carrying the weight of past hurts that had closed his heart. Through the path's guidance, he had found the strength to forgive, to release his pain and allow compassion to take root in his heart. He had learned that forgiveness was a gift he could give himself, a way of finding freedom and peace.

Maya felt a sense of awe as she listened to Johan's story, understanding that compassion was a source of healing, a way of releasing the burdens of anger and resentment. She realized that compassion allowed people to let go of pain, to find a sense of peace and acceptance that opened the heart.

They continued along the path, and Sari shared more stories, each one a testament to the power of compassion. She spoke of a young girl who had come to the path feeling lonely and isolated, struggling to connect with others. Through the path's gentle encouragement, she had found compassion for those around her, learning to see beyond her own struggles and offer kindness and understanding to others. In doing so, she had created friendships and connections that filled her heart with joy.

Maya felt a warmth spreading through her as she listened, understanding that compassion was a bridge that connected people, a way of breaking down walls and creating bonds. She realized that compassion was a way of seeing others, of recognizing their pain and joys, and responding with kindness and understanding.

As they walked further, they came upon a family who had come to the path to find unity and understanding. The parents shared how they often brought their children here to teach them about compassion, about the importance of kindness and empathy. They spoke of how compassion had strengthened their family, creating a bond of love and support that carried them through life's challenges.

Maya watched as the family sat together, their faces filled with love and understanding. She realized that compassion was not only an individual journey; it was something that could bring people together, creating a sense of unity and belonging. She felt a newfound appreciation for the power of compassion, for the way it fostered connection and harmony.

As the day continued, Sari led her to a small garden where stones were arranged in a spiral pattern. Each stone was engraved with words of compassion—phrases like "You are loved," "Forgive freely," and "Kindness heals." Sari explained that these stones had been placed there by those who had walked the path before her, each one a reminder of the strength and beauty of compassion.

Chapter 25: The Horizon of Unity

Each journey, every adventure, had led Maya to places of beauty and understanding. She had met wise guides and compassionate souls, all of whom had shared with her the profound lessons that now rested deeply within her heart. As she turned to the next page, she saw an illustration of a vast horizon stretching endlessly, where the land met the sky. The horizon was bathed in the warm glow of the setting sun, with colors blending seamlessly into one another, as if the earth and heavens were united in perfect harmony. Maya felt a sense of peace and belonging as she looked at the horizon, a feeling that she was connected to something larger, something universal. In the next moment, she felt herself standing on the edge of that very horizon.

The landscape around her was serene, filled with open fields dotted with wildflowers in every shade imaginable, swaying gently in the breeze. The air was calm and filled with the faint hum of nature—a chorus of birds, the rustle of grass, and the quiet murmur of life moving in harmony. Maya took a deep breath, feeling the peace of the place settle over her, as if the world itself was welcoming her home.

"Welcome, Maya," a voice called softly. She turned to see an elderly woman approaching her, her face wise and serene, her eyes filled with a gentle warmth that seemed to hold a thousand stories. The woman wore simple, flowing robes that seemed to blend with the colors of the horizon, and her presence radiated a quiet strength, as if she was both grounded in the earth and connected to the sky.

"My name is Amara," the woman said with a smile. "I am the Keeper of the Horizon of Unity. This horizon is a place where people come to understand their connection to all things, to feel the unity that binds us to each other, to the earth, and to the universe."

Maya felt a deep respect for Amara, sensing her calm wisdom and her gentle understanding of the world. "What does it mean to be united?" she asked, her voice filled with wonder.

Amara's smile softened, and she gestured to the horizon before them. "Unity is the understanding that we are all connected, that each life, each heart, is part of a greater whole. Unity is the harmony that exists when we see ourselves in others, when we recognize that every being, every soul, is linked by the same thread of life. To embrace unity is to embrace the world with love, to see beyond differences and divisions, and to honor the beauty that exists in every person, every creature, every element."

Maya nodded, feeling the truth of Amara's words settle within her. She looked out at the horizon, noticing how the sky and the earth seemed to blend together, their colors merging to form a seamless tapestry. She realized that unity was like the horizon itself, a point where everything came together, where differences were woven into a single, beautiful whole.

Amara began to walk along the horizon, and Maya followed, her heart open and her mind calm. As they walked, Amara shared stories of unity, tales of people who had come to the horizon seeking connection, understanding, and peace. She spoke of a young man who had felt isolated and alone, unable to see his place in the world. Through the horizon's quiet guidance, he had learned to recognize the beauty in others, to see himself in the lives around him, and to understand that he was never truly alone. In unity, he had found belonging and strength, realizing that he was part of a larger story, a shared journey that bound him to every life.

Maya listened, feeling a deep admiration for the young man's journey. She thought about her own life, the moments when she had felt disconnected or uncertain, and how each adventure within the book had shown her that she was part of something larger. She realized that unity wasn't about losing herself but about finding herself in the greater tapestry of existence, about understanding that each thread was unique and vital to the whole.

As they continued walking, they came upon a family seated together, their faces filled with warmth and joy. The parents were sharing stories with their children, each tale bringing smiles and laughter, their voices harmonizing like a gentle song. Amara explained that the family often came to the horizon to find peace, to feel the connection that bound them to each other and to the world around them.

Maya watched as the family laughed and shared together, understanding that unity was not only about individual lives but about the bonds that connected people to one another. She realized that unity was about family, friendship, and community, about the love and trust that brought people together. She felt a newfound appreciation for the beauty of these connections, for the way unity created a sense of belonging and joy.

As they walked further, Amara shared more stories, each one a testament to the power of unity. She spoke of a healer who had come to the horizon, seeking strength and guidance as she faced challenges in her work. Through the horizon's quiet encouragement, she had come to understand that her healing was not something she did alone; it was a collaboration, a partnership with the people she served and the universe itself. She had learned to see each person she healed as a part of herself, each life as a reflection of her own heart.

Amara led her to a small circle of stones, each one engraved with words of unity—phrases like "We are one," "Together we rise," and "In harmony, we thrive." Amara explained that these stones had been placed by those who had come to the horizon before her, each one a reminder of the beauty and power of unity.

Don't miss out!

Visit the website below and you can sign up to receive emails whenever Maya Roberts publishes a new book. There's no charge and no obligation.

https://books2read.com/r/B-A-MLLVC-YSOIF

BOOKS2READ

Connecting independent readers to independent writers.

Did you love *The Book of Endless Stories*? Then you should read *The Friendship Tree*[1] by Isaac Lewis!

The Friendship Tree tells the heartwarming story of four friends who plant a tree together, each bringing soil from their home. Through seasons of growth, change, and connection, the tree becomes a powerful symbol of friendship, unity, and love for generations. As the children grow, so does the tree, weaving the memories of many into its roots and branches. With each chapter, readers explore the power of kindness, respect, and community in shaping lives and creating lasting legacies. This book celebrates friendship in its many forms, inspiring young readers to cherish the connections they make and nurture them.

---

1. https://books2read.com/u/38qJ17

2. https://books2read.com/u/38qJ17

About the Publisher

Whimsy Tales Press is a creative powerhouse devoted to publishing exceptional children's books that spark joy, imagination, and lifelong learning. With a mission to inspire young minds, the company crafts stories that celebrate diversity, kindness, and the magic of discovery. Whimsy Tales Press collaborates with passionate authors and illustrators to bring captivating characters and enchanting worlds to life. From heartwarming bedtime tales to empowering adventures, every book is designed to entertain while fostering empathy and curiosity. Committed to excellence and inclusivity, Whimsy Tales Press ensures that each story leaves a lasting impression, encouraging children to dream big and believe in endless possibilities.

Milton Keynes UK
Ingram Content Group UK Ltd.
UKHW020914291124
451807UK00013B/922